SWORDS
BOOK FIVE OF THE

Robert Ryan

Copyright © 2023 Robert J. Ryan
All Rights Reserved. The right of Robert J. Ryan to be
identified as the author of this work has been asserted.
All of the characters in this book are fictitious and any
resemblance to actual persons, living or dead, is coincidental.

Cover design by www.damonza.com

ISBN: 9798375462097
(print edition)

Trotting Fox Press

Contents

1. By all the Powers	3
2. A Time for Names	13
3. Battle and Blood	21
4. Let Me Through!	32
5. Reunited	38
6. He Is a Dead Man	45
7. A Red Mist	52
8. Stalemate	62
9. The Mach Furr	69
10. So Be It	73
11. A Tear in Reality	80
12. Voices in The Mist	87
13. Voices of Entrapment	96
14. A Glance Full of Evil	106
15. The Silent Enemy	111
16. Touch the Swords	120
17. Rise, and Be Ready	132
18. We Must Be Swift!	137
19. The Gathering of the Tribes	146
20. A Poisoned Blade	154
21. The Game of Nobility	167
22. I Have Done It Before	173
23. A Ghostly Image	179
Appendix: Encyclopedic Glossary	192

1. By all the Powers

The mist swirled ahead. It signaled to Shar that the enchanted barrier hemming in the valley was close. Just as close was the moment of truth where she would discover if the shamans she had gone to so much trouble to find would betray her.

Her wound ached. It was not deep, and the sword of Cragamasta had only cut a finger's width into her flesh, but it had done so on her stomach and every step she took irritated it.

She strode ahead, following the shamans who, despite their age, set a fast pace. They were inscrutable, and though they had said and done all the right things since she had survived their test, she mistrusted them. Trust had to be won by action, and they had not done so yet. Only when they were free of this valley would she know the truth in their hearts, for then they would be free to kill her if they chose. They were too many for her and her companions to fight.

Yet a day ago, they had hailed her as Nakatath, emperor-to-be, after her victory against Cragamasta. It had been a strange moment. The words of the god still echoed in her ear, for he had said things that gave her both great hope and great fear. The shamans had tended her, taking her into their great hall and applying a soothing balm to her wound and dressing it in clean bandages. They seemed to accept the outcome of the contest between her and Cragamasta without surprise, just as they might have accepted the winner of a coin toss.

It had been more than that though. She still did not know how she had won. Perhaps it was her fate. Or the prophecy of Chen Fei at work, as though it were somehow magic and able to shape events. Or maybe it was just pure luck. She should not have though, and it troubled her.

She had been wrong. Coming to this valley was a risk too high to take, and she should have found another way. She vowed not to make that mistake again, but instantly knew that circumstances might once more force her to take such a chance in the future.

The mists swirled ahead, and the shamans slowed. They did not seem to like it here. Perhaps the mist was a reminder of the great magic that had trapped them.

"They are nervous," Huigar whispered from close by.

"As am I," Shar replied.

Asana seemed calm as usual. He walked with his head slightly bowed as though deep in thought. Probably, like her, he was weighing up in his mind what the shamans would do when they were free of the valley.

She was wrong though. She saw that instantly when he glanced up at her, and something came into his gaze that she had never seen before. He looked at her strangely, and she knew he was thinking of her.

"How did you win?" he asked. "You're very good with a sword, but the god was better."

"My life belongs to the empire," she replied. "Not to the gods."

It was as good an answer as any. She did not quite believe it herself, but she was not sure it was wrong either. Whatever the case, she did not wish to show her own doubts. Not now when she must be strong.

They came closer to the crest of the ridge where there would be more stone pillars such as the ones where Shar had gained entry to the valley. The afternoon was wearing on, and the once-blue sky was growing gray as afternoon shadows tumbled down the slope behind them.

She walked ahead a little faster, and got the attention of one of the shamans.

"I would speak for a little to the elder who leads you all," she said. "There's something to discuss before we leave the valley."

The shaman offered a bow, gave no sign of his thoughts, and went to fetch his leader.

Whether by some command that she did not see, or merely by seeing the elder walk back in her direction, the entire group came to a stop. Just as well, too. At that moment the mist drew back a little, and Shar saw a great pillar of stone rise up to the sky before the mist rolled over it again. They were nearly at journey's end. At least inside the valley.

The old man came before her, and leaned on his staff. His straggly white hair and withered hands made him look ancient and frail. Yet he had climbed the slope as swiftly as the others.

"What may I do for you?" he asked.

"You tested me to see if I was worthy of following," she replied.

The old man inclined his head. "We did."

"I don't blame you for that. You have a right to know the character of any you serve, and if they have the intelligence and courage to lead you."

He gave no answer, but his eyes gazed into hers as though he could read her soul. She had the feeling he knew what she was going to ask.

"A leader must also test those who follow. Will they be loyal? Will they be trustworthy? Is that not fair?"

"It is. You may test us, and we will not hold it against you any more than you hold it against us. We are ready."

"This then, is what I wish. Swear the Great Oath as was used in the Shadowed Wars. Swear you will serve me truly. You, and all your companions."

The Great Oath was no light thing to ask. No more profound pledge existed. Even so, the old man merely nodded and called the shamans to gather round him.

"We will swear the Great Oath," he said in a loud voice. "Are there any that choose not to?"

There was silence, and Shar realized they had expected this. No doubt, over the time of their imprisonment, they would have had endless discussions about what would be asked of them, and what they would do or refuse.

It was disconcerting to Shar to discover such a thing, for she strove not to be predictable. Any enemy who knew what she might do next was one that could beat her. She was playing a game with these shamans where every move she made had been considered by them before she was even born.

The old man gripped tight his staff and raised it into the air. A light, faint yet steady, burned at the tip. All the others did likewise.

"We pledge to follow Shar Fei," the old man said, and the others echoed his words. "We will serve her truly and faithfully until such time as she has beaten her enemies or they have beaten her. We will obey her commands, and give advice that can be trusted. We swear these things by all the powers that move and substance the earth. May death strike us down if we break our bond!"

As the old man spoke the last words, light flared at the tip of each staff, and a brightness shone forth. Shar felt a thrum through the scabbards of her swords, and she knew they responded to some magic. The Great Oath was like that. It called forth the land itself as a witness.

Even so, Shar still felt mistrust. The oath could be broken, but it was rarely done and there were stories of those who had. They died afterward by some strange circumstance. Superstition maybe, but one the shamans might choose to test.

She bowed to them. "Then let us proceed. The way out, that you have long awaited, is at hand."

Shar walked now with an eager step. The shamans seemed to catch something of her mood, for they quickened their pace as well. It was only natural that they were keen to leave this place, but until now they had kept the veiled air of shamans about them. *The shaman who shows their thought is not a true shaman*, as the old proverb went.

The mist rolled down the last of the slope to meet them, and along its edge they entered a small wood. It was quiet and subdued here. Almost, Shar could feel magic in the air. Then she remembered that there might well be an older magic in this valley than the one Shulu had set as a trap.

The wood was dark. It was mostly of stunted oaks, for here the soil was thin, and the trees looked like staggering men, limbs reaching out and groping.

Shar tripped over a root, and looking down she was surprised to see that the shamans now led the way forward over a path. Swiftly, she knew why.

Looking ahead there was a small clearing, and in the center of it was the trunk of a tree, larger than the rest. The top was gone, having long since rotted into the earth, but the roots and stump, man high, remained.

The shamans slowed, and offered a deep bow to it as though it were alive. Then they walked on. When Shar drew closer she saw that the stump had been carved. In some ways the art was primitive, for it looked to have been done with an axe, yet despite that there was a certain sense of perfect realness to it. In the dim light and misty air, it seemed that a man stood there.

It was not any man though. She had seen the image of Chen Fei, and this was true to it. Now, she even saw lines in the timber that suggested sheathed swords at the figure's side, and there was no mistaking the eyes. They were painted violet.

"You should not be surprised," the old man said who led the shamans. "We revered Chen Fei. We crafted this to honor him."

"And yet you betrayed him."

The shaman nodded slowly. "We did. And we paid the price for it. Know, however, that we are not on the side of those shamans that are your enemies. Nor are we on your side. We serve the land. Yet, as we have sworn, we will serve you truly until our oath no longer binds us."

They passed through the wood in silence then, and when they came to the other side night was falling and the mist grew into a thick fog. The shamans used magic to light several branches, which they held aloft as the procession moved to the ridge of the valley.

Out of the gray, two pillars emerged. They too were gray, but moisture slicked the surface of the stone blocks that formed them and gave them a darker cast.

The shamans stood still, and Shar readied herself. Once the enchantment that formed this trap was undone, it could not be reinstated. The shamans were free forever, and her enemies from outside could find her. At least on that count she felt confident. They would not have had time to surround the valley, nor could they know at what point she would emerge. Yet they had found her before, and it would not take them long to do so again. She must get to Chatchek Fortress quickly.

She strode forward, drawing her swords as she walked. She felt the hilts thrum within her hand. The magic of the pillars had woken them from slumber, and there was almost a sense of expectation.

Shar did not pursue that thought. No good would come from sensing the swords too deeply. She knew what was in them.

She knew what was in the pillars also, and the enchantment that she was about to break would set the demons free. So Shulu had told her, but she had also said that they could do no harm and must return to their own dark realm. So she had said, but how much did even Shulu know of these matters that were the province of the gods and beyond the understanding of humanity?

"Do not fear," Shar told the shamans. "You will see that which will make you tremble, but you are safe."

She hoped she had not just uttered a lie.

The stone of the pillar was clammy to touch, and she did not like the feel of it. Yet she ran her hand over the surface and found the two notches she was looking for. They were hard to see, and by some cunning of craftsmanship looked like nothing more than an area where the stone had flaked.

Drawing the Swords of Dawn and Dusk, she found those crevices with the points and slowly drove the blades home. They penetrated full depth into the stone, until only the hilts were visible, and then she uttered the words of power that Shulu had taught her.

Nothing happened. Then a wind blew from outside the valley and tore at the fog, dispersing it and allowing the cold stars to twinkle in the twilight sky. The earth trembled, and the wind changed direction, now flowing back up the slope and moaning over the ridge.

Shar withdrew the swords, and a pale blue flame ran along their lengths. She did not sheath them, but stood back and assumed a fighting stance. In truth, she was not exactly sure what would happen next.

The shamans uncharacteristically let out a wild yell, for they sensed they were free at last. Magic filled the air, and blue light flashed from the tops of the pillars and ringed the valley as though strange lightning leaped to fence in the entire vale.

The earth rumbled, and the pillars swayed. Then a terrible stillness descended. The quiet was welcome, yet Shar sensed there was something more to come.

The light flared again, ringing the valley, then it drew to the center of the sky above in a multitude of hues. And it was no longer light.

Seven figures hung there, enormous and horrible. They were the demons that had formed the enchantment, and now they were free of it.

The figures swelled with power, and Shar felt the swords in her hands respond. They flared with a bright light, and the demons in the air swooped down toward the small group of humanity.

Shar stepped forward to meet them, swords high before her. Asana was at her side, and then Huigar and Radatan. The shamans seemed caught by surprise, for they did nothing. But then their leader stepped up next to Shar, his staff high and held tightly in his withered hands.

The demons plunged downward, and there was a roar in the air.

"Hail brothers!" came the strange voice from the Swords of Dawn and Dusk.

"We are free!" cried the seven demons as one.

They drew close, and their terrible features were visible. One had hair of fire that streamed behind it. Another, horned and winged, gnashed terrible fangs.

Then the demons cried out. "No!" And their voices were filled with anguish. Like an arrow shot from a bow and reaching the zenith of its flight, they began to plummet. No longer did they head for the group of humanity, but instead plunged straight down. The earth fissured before them, and through this rent they fell, raging. Then the earth closed over them, and it was quiet again.

"From hell they came," the leader of the shamans whispered, "and to hell they return."

Shar sensed how much the old man was shaken. So were the other shamans. As much as they had foreknown things about her, it was clear they had not guessed the nature of the magic imprisoning them. Nor of the Swords of Dawn and Dusk.

"I cannot believe it," the old man said. "Whence did the knowledge of such magic come? Whence the audacity to use it?"

Shar was not about to tell him more, at least the little of it that she knew.

"You are free," she said. "Come! See the outside world that you have not beheld in a thousand years."

This time she led the way, walking past the perimeter of the pillars. She stayed clear of them, for they no longer stood upright but leaned as though they might fall.

Straightaway she knew something was wrong. She could not tell what. It was twilight as before, but the stars seemed to be fading rather than growing brighter. And the air felt different, somehow. Then she understood. They had left not just the enclosure of magic, but had also entered a different time. It was not the twilight of dusk about her, but the dawn of a new day.

The sun rose, casting golden spears of light over the land. After the demons she appreciated anew the glory and beauty of such a simple thing.

Yet her life was not so simple. The shamans were free now. Her footsteps had turned downhill, and they were outside the valley. She turned and looked at them, ready for anything but knowing, if they broke their oath, they were stronger than she and her companions combined. By far.

In silence, she waited.

2. A Time for Names

Shar's companions sensed this was a moment of great danger as well, and Asana, Huigar and Radatan drew close. Shar forgot the beauty of the dawn, and waited with a tenseness she hoped she hid.

The shamans looked around, almost bewildered, yet with a growing sense of joy. They did not look like they had any plan to attack, or to just walk away.

After a little while, the old man who led them approached. He guessed Shar's concern, or so it seemed.

"We will keep our oath, Nakatath. Have no fear. We will serve you, for the moment at least. And when our oath no longer constrains us, then we will see."

It was the best she could hope for, and in truth it was a great asset to her. With allies such as these, she had a chance of defending her rebellion against the magic of the shamans. Even so, it would do no one any good if they were not there. Suddenly, she ached to be back with her army. By now, they should be in Chatchek Fortress. Yet they could be hard pressed by the enemy. If so, and the shamans unleashed their powers, the rebellion could be crushed. She felt a great urgency to reach them, but then quelled it. She had achieved her quest, and she could do no more. It would take days to get there, and nothing would change that.

The old man leaned on his staff, and studied her. "It is a time for names now," he said. "We know yours but you do not know ours. We will be companions, for a while at least, and it is time for our formality to cease."

"I'd welcome that," Shar replied.

The old man held out his hand. "I am called Ravengrim."

Shar took his hand and shook it. It was a strange name, and not Cheng at all.

The other two elders approached, having heard what was said.

"This," Ravengrim told her, "is Wolfshadow."

Shar shook hands with the man. He had been cold to her at their first meeting back in the hall. It did not seem that his attitude had changed much, but perhaps it had thawed a little.

"And this," Ravengrim continued, "is Runeguard."

It was another cold handshake. Shar did not mind. It would be too much to expect these people to like her. All that was required was that they held to their word, and that it seemed they would do. Of them all, only Ravengrim seemed to enjoy her company. He had, perhaps, been the harshest of them all at their first meeting, but in his case he was doing his duty and testing her. Underneath, she had sensed he held no dislike for her, and now, with time, he seemed to be showing her some friendship. Mistrustful as she was, she would not refuse it.

"We had best hurry," Shar said. "The enemy will be seeking us, and though the distance to Chatchek Fortress is not that great, the sooner we get there the safer we'll be."

Ravengrim did not seem in the least concerned, nevertheless they hastened on. It was true that Shar had a lot less to fear now. With fifty shamans to guard her, no attack by wolves or the like was a threat. Even so, fifty shamans could only do so much against a force of shamans of about the same number. Her enemies could raise such a force against her many times over.

They were a strange group of shamans, and Shar did not wish to think of them as such. The shamans were her enemies, and for all that these people possessed the use of magic, they were different. They looked different, their names were of foreign origin, perhaps coming from Duthenor lands, and they acted differently.

"What shall I call you all," Shar asked Ravengrim. "Together, I mean. You're shamans, but you're not like the ones that rule over the land now."

"No, we are not. Not back in your forefather's day, nor now it seems." The old man looked away from her and his eyes grew distant as though he thought intently of that far off time. "Chen Fei called us his *Nahat*. We will go by that designation again."

Shar liked it. It meant fifty, but it held a connotation of more than that. It was a term used to signify something special such as a fifty-year anniversary.

They moved ahead then, striking out northward and toward Chatchek Fortress. Shar could not help considering these strange new allies. They had names that were likely from Duthenor lands, or close by. They dressed and appeared as though their ancestry was only partially Cheng. Yet at the same time they spoke the Cheng language perfectly, even if with an archaic flavor. And the term Nahat could not be more Cheng. It was not just used as a term of ceremony, but also, so Shulu had told her, that in Chen Fei's time battalions were often formed of fifty soldiers and called nahat-nitra, which meant fifty swords.

Ravengrim walked with her at times, and he sometimes did so in silence while at others talked quite freely as though he had known her for a long time.

"This Chatchek Fortress that we go to, was it not destroyed?"

"It was taken by the emperor, and damaged. But not destroyed."

Shar felt strange telling him that. He should have known more about it than she did, but the Nahat must have joined him at some time after that campaign. He surprised her though, for he obviously knew something about the fortress even if he was not there at the battle when it fell.

"It was an old, old fortress even in my time. There is magic in the stones on which it was built, even as there is magic in the valley behind us. Ancient magic, and not of the making of shamans."

"I don't fear the magic," Radatan said. "I fear we'll find our army there, already surrounded by the enemy."

Shar worried about that too. She had not sent Kubodin there without thinking of such a thing though. If worst came to worst, there would be a way into the fortress from the rugged hills at the back. It would take the enemy quite a while to cut that route off.

"You *should* fear the magic," Ravengrim said. There was something in his tone that suggested he knew far more than he said, but he went on before Shar could ask. "As to the fortress being surrounded, the Nahat will give thought to that."

They moved swiftly across the land, and it was country that Shar was familiar with. She had been here before, or close to it, when on the Quest of Swords before she had claimed her birthright.

A cold wind blew from the north, driving harder and fading away by turns. There was a bite of winter in it, and Shar fancied she could smell snow on it, but it was not cold enough for that. At least not yet, nor for a little while. It was coming soon though, and that was both a fear and a hope. The enemy, not having a fortress in which to shelter, would suffer greatly through the weather. Yet it might drive them all the faster to some terrible magic in order to try to quell the rebellion. One that might succeed despite her having the Nahat.

They camped in a small stand of trees, and the wind howled through the leaves much of the night. By dawn though, it faded to a breeze and the sun rose into a cloudless sky and swiftly heated the air.

Of the enemy, there had so far been no sign.

That changed. They marched again, and they had only had their first rest break when Huigar pointed skyward.

"The ibis are back," she said.

Shar studied them. There was a group of ten or so, drifting in slow circles high in the sky. It seemed to her that it was too late in the season for them to be present. They should have migrated southward, to warmer climates, by now.

She glanced at Ravengrim, who was standing nearby and looking a little puzzled.

"That's how the shamans found us last time, before we entered Nathradin Valley. At least, so we think."

Ravengrim shielded his eyes with a hand and studied them for a few moments.

"It could be," he said. "It is no threat to us, but I can see if it is so and do something about it, if you like."

Shar thought he was overconfident. There might be fifty shamans here, and they were a match for a small army. But the enemy had the resources to send several armies against them if circumstances allowed. All that it required was for troops to be in the vicinity, and that was certainly possible.

"Do what you can," she said. "In the past, we traveled by night to try to avoid being seen, but I dare not tarry like that now. We have to get to Chatchek quickly."

"Very well," the old man agreed. His eyes grew vacant then, yet nothing happened for several minutes.

At length, Radatan pointed to the north. "Over there."

Shar looked in that direction. She saw nothing but the sky at first, then she observed a tiny dot. Whatever kind of bird it was, it had climbed high in the air and was barely visible. Then, as it drew closer to the group of people, and the ibis that were above them, she saw that it was a hawk.

The hawk was above the ibis too, and suddenly it stooped and plummeted at tremendous speed into their midst. The ibis awkwardly separated, not prepared by nature for defense against attacking hawks, for they were too big to be hunted.

Chaos broke out in the sky, and the ibis flapped their wings quickly in contrast to the slow gliding of before. They were soon out of danger though, and slowed down again. Except for one.

The hawk fixed on a single ibis, driving it closely from behind, yet not ripping it with its talons as it might have done.

Shar understood. Ravengrim had melded his mind with the hawk, and he had sensed which ibis was similarly controlled by a shaman. Yet he did not wish to kill the bird, and that pleased her. It showed he had compassion, and it was enough to make the shaman let loose its control of the creature.

The ibis suddenly tumbled in the air as though dead in midflight. The hawk had not touched it. Then it righted itself and winged away. The hawk too seemed to lose all interest in it, and with a few quick strokes of it wings it angled off in a different direction.

Shar looked at Ravengrim. The man's eyes were still momentarily vacant, then they came to life again, and he laughed.

"An interesting game!" he said. "One I have not played in a very long time."

"And the shaman?" Shar asked.

Ravengrim grew sober. "There was one only. He fled back to his body, as well he might. If he represented these modern-day shamans in power, we have little to fear."

Again, there was that overconfidence, and Shar did not like it. Still, it might be that the shamans had diminished in power over the great period of time since Chen Fei last tested them. At least, the newer ones. Shar suspected though that the shaman elders would be a match for the Nahat.

They had no further trouble from the enemy as they traveled, and several days and nights passed without incident. The cold wind renewed itself, and they struggled into it at times when it blew hard, but it slowly diminished until it was still and the sky became overcast, but without rain.

The countryside changed, and Shar knew they were close to Chatchek now. They veered a little to the left, not wishing to set a direct route to their destination so as to avoid any ambush set for them by the shamans. They had not been seen since the ibis, but that was no guarantee that the shamans did not know where Shar was heading. By now, Kubodin must have occupied the fortress, and the plan to winter there would be obvious. So too that Shar would join them.

They smelled smoke in the air on the last night, and Shar did not like it. Perhaps it was the cooking fires in Chatchek Fortress, and all it signified was that her army was being fed. She feared though that it was the enemy who had invested the fortress, surrounding it, or trying to, in order to ensure no one entered or escaped.

So it was proved early the next day. Traveling with great caution to avoid being seen from the air or by scouts, they came within sight of the fortress. A massive army was camped before it.

They drew closer, using a small wood to conceal themselves, and looked out in silence for some time.

"Well, it's going to be harder for us to get inside there than for a dog not to bark at a cat," Radatan said.

3. Battle and Blood

Kubodin watched the battle with detachment.

His hands itched to take up his axe and fight instead of watching others risk their lives and die. His mind rebelled at looking at it all as a cold calculation, instead of feeling the searing emotions he held at bay.

Neither was his role though. He had command, and he best served his army by being detached and making correct decisions at the right time.

"Over there!" Nahring called out.

Kubodin had seen it too. The tower in which he stood gave a perfect view of the entire length of the rampart below. Enemy soldiers had climbed up by ropes attached to grappling hooks, and made the top of the rampart. Hundreds of their comrades had fallen attempting the same thing. The defenders were good now at their job, and they had the advantage. Sooner or later though, it was expected some would break through.

"Shall I send reinforcements, sir?" It was one of his aides who asked the question. Kubodin had found he needed many in order to communicate well with different sections of the army. At any given time, most were going to or coming back from a task.

He shook his head, giving that as his only answer while he watched intently. The aides were younger men, and they had not yet hardened up as he had. To send reinforcements every time a problem occurred was to train the soldiers to rely on getting help. A time would come when there would be no help to give, and it was better they learned to rally themselves and fight back.

So it proved here. More of the enemy made it to the ramparts, and Kubodin watched in silence as some of his own men were slain. Then a Green Hornet warrior, at least Kubodin thought he was, got behind them and severed the already damaged rope with a great swing of his axe. Kubodin heard the thud of it biting into the stone even above the general din of battle.

The enemy on the rampart was cut off from retreat. Perhaps, they could have tried to surrender, but they did not. One of them let out a wild yell and drove forward into the defenders, killing a soldier and wounding another. His comrades, less vocal than he, were just as brave. They too laid about them, and for a moment they seemed unstoppable.

Numbers counted though, and the defenders were far more numerous. First one of the attackers fell, and then the rest. Their bodies were heaved over the ramparts as missiles to dislodge the enemy climbing up on ropes and ladders nearby.

Kubodin continued to watch in silence, yet his warrior heart was stirred. Those men had been brave, and whether they were enemies or not did not change it. They deserved a better fate than they got, and it was the shamans who were ultimately responsible for this bloodshed among the tribes. They were the root of the evil, and warriors, for the most part, just fought and died according to the dictates of their leaders.

One of the aides called out. "Look at that!"

Kubodin saw. A dead man had been picked up, and the defender who did it staggered with him toward the ramparts. Yet the attacker was *not* dead. It was the man who had led the assault just moments ago. His helm had been knocked off. Blood covered his face. Several deep wounds pierced his body, and he was covered in blood. He should have been dead, but perhaps he had only been knocked out. Yet he began to struggle, and even as they reached the ledge he managed to get his feet on the ground.

There the two men wrestled. The wounded man could not win though, and already defenders were approaching to kill him once and for all. With a final mighty effort, the attacker, mortally wounded as he was and in his death throes, grabbed hold of the defender in a grip that could not be broken and dragged them both over the rampart to topple toward oblivion below.

Kubodin averted his eyes. It was an act of bravery such as all warriors understood, no matter whom they fought for. He did not hate the attacker for it. Yet the blood that was being spilled today … that would be spilled hereafter, it was a waste of the finest men of the empire.

"They'll retreat now," Kubodin said. The aides looked at him strangely, for the fighting seemed at its thickest just then. Nahring glanced at him, but said nothing. The other chief likely thought the same thing, but was not quite as sure. Those who had fought in battles, and watched them, could read them as though they were a book and guess something of what was to come before the pages were turned.

The enemy seemed full of fighting spirit, but within a few moments the battle turned against them and their spirits sagged like a sail without wind in it. Horns were sounded, and their retreat ordered. The enemy fled to jeers from those who defended the walls, and they looked dispirited and beaten.

"How did you know?" one of the aides asked in surprise.

"When they broke through onto the rampart they thought they might overrun the fortress. But that sally was beaten back, and they were returned to the position they held at the start. The only difference was hundreds of dead men. Nothing daunts more than a total lack of progress despite hard work."

Nahring nodded. "But they'll learn greater endurance with time. And the shamans will drive them all the harder."

That was certainly true, and Kubodin acknowledged it with a nod. However strong the fortress was, they would struggle to hold it over the long term. The enemy had too much to throw at them. What worried him more though was that the shamans would not wait that long. His thoughts drifted to Shar. Only in her was there hope. In her, and the help he hoped she could bring.

Reports came in swiftly now as different areas on the rampart sent the numbers of their killed and injured. It was mostly as expected. One young messenger, a Green Hornet warrior, had tears in his eyes though when he approached.

"What is it, lad?" Kubodin asked.

The young man steadied himself, but grief was in his eyes.

"Our chief is dead. He was killed when the enemy broke through on the rampart."

Kubodin placed a hand on the young man's shoulder. "I'm sorry to hear that. He died valiantly then, for that was some hard fighting. It was not in vain though. He, and your tribe fighting there, taught the enemy to fear us."

Nahring offered the young man some water, and then the two chiefs watched as the soldier walked away listlessly.

"Who will be the next Green Hornet chief?" Nahring asked.

"That's a problem for Shar," Kubodin said. "Only she has the authority to appoint a chief."

"Unless the Green Hornets decide to appoint their own. The tribes are used to doing that."

Kubodin was not sure if they would still do so. The Green Hornets had been reluctant to join Shar at first, but they had proved themselves many times since then, not least today.

"We'll see," he replied. If they did, it might cause problems. What if the new chief was less supportive of Shar?

More and more reports came in, and Kubodin was as pleased as was possible under the circumstances. It was true that Shar's army had lost men, but the devastation to the enemy was massive. No longer did warriors mutter against fighting behind walls. Now they loved it, and they loved Shar even more.

The hours passed in anxiety. There would be another attack today. The enemy showed all signs of preparing for one, and there was time enough left in the day for it. Kubodin felt confident they would repel it though. That opinion was shared by all of Shar's army. Yet waiting for it was a mental torture.

"Why do they take so long?" Dakashul asked. The Iron Dog chief had joined Kubodin and Nahring had gone to walk the ramparts and talk to the men.

"Perhaps they want us to feel this way," Kubodin replied. "The battles fought in our imaginations are more draining than the real ones. At least the real ones have a beginning and end."

"Humph!" Dakashul clenched his fist and scowled out from the top of the tower at the thousands gathered below. "That's shamans for you. They plan. They scheme. They plot. A proper man just puts a knife in your belly and is done with it."

There was a certain truth to that, but the simple approach of tribesmen was coming to an end. Kubodin was not sure he liked it either. But change was coming to the lands of the Cheng, whether they liked it or not. Even if Shar lost, things would no longer return to the way they had been. The clans had learned what it was to fight together instead of against each other. They would not forget easily.

The attack finally came. A mass of the enemy surged forward in a rolling march. With them were soldiers carrying grappling hooks and ladders. Shield bearers were with them to protect those assets. The warriors had to take their own chances against the arrows and spears that rained death upon them though, for the Nagraks were used to mounted fighting where they held a saber in one hand and their pony's reins in the other. Shields were uncommon in the clan.

Dakashul leaned out over the tower battlement, and his gaze was fierce.

"I hope we kill them all! But by the heavens, there are a lot of them!"

"We'll beat them back again," Kubodin replied. "But what then? The more we defeat them, the more the shamans will be driven to use magic."

The other chief did not take his intense gaze off the enemy.

"Maybe so, but surely they'll be reluctant to do that. No warrior will respect them after that, and it might be the fastest way to have the Nagraks join the rebellion."

Kubodin wished to believe that, but he did not think it would unfold that way. As much as the Nagraks would dislike it, they were at the heart of the shamans' rule. There were more that supported them than among any other tribe, or at least so rumor declared, and the shamans, if they could not count on loyalty would count on fear. Whatever magic they used against the rebellion could be turned upon the Nagraks just as easily, and they would know it.

The advancing army crashed into the rampart in a thunder of war cries and screams. Grappling hooks were thrown up. Arrows and spears were hurled down. And the air was drenched with desperation as men fought men for the continuation of their very lives.

Despite all the death, the enemy swarmed up the side of the battlement like thousands of ants. Grappling ropes were cut, but it was harder this time. They had relearned some of the skills of their ancestors, and the ropes were now twined with wire that made cutting them harder. Yet still they were cut, and the ladders were toppled sending men screaming to their deaths below. Or injured, which Kubodin grimly calculated to be worse. The injured must be cared for and fed, and that would drain the resources of the enemy more swiftly. Disease might also be more likely to spread, especially with winter coming on.

The fighting raged below, for now not just the front of the wall was contested but in several places the enemy had reached the top of the side battlements. Fighting was fiercest there, and Kubodin wished to rush down from the tower and help.

Instead, he gazed coolly from his higher vantage. His was the responsibility of command, and he must detach himself from emotion and make decisions only. Unless the shamans used sorcery. What he could do then, he did not know. He was the only one who might act against it though.

The axe hanging down through his belt called to him. It sensed the bloodshed, and it was eager to join. He did not know how he knew that, but he knew. His hand slid down to touch the blades. *Soon. You will taste blood soon.*

The axe did not answer, but the eagerness diminished. It was only then that Kubodin realized he had spoken to his weapon, and he did not like that. He knew what was in the blades, and he knew madness waited for him if the axe began to control him. He should cast it away, yet it was needed. Now more than ever, and he was defenseless without it, against men or magic. He *needed* it.

The battlement ran red with blood, and the screams of the men as they were hacked to death tore at the air. Ally or foe, it was a terrible sound to hear. Then something rose above it, and Kubodin was stunned.

Strangely, the men began to sing. He was not sure where it started, but others took it up and it grew louder. He was not sure if it was the defenders or the attackers. He was not sure what it signified. It was eerie and disconcerting.

Soon he began to pick out the words though. It was a song sometimes sung around a campfire, late at night. It was a ballad of the Shadowed Wars, and men had voiced it as they faced battle and death. It spoke of the fleeting nature of life, but the everlasting spirit of humanity that strove to bring light to the dark.

It was his men that sung it, he realized. Their voices swelled and rolled like the ocean, unstoppable. It drowned out the terrible sounds of killing, and the defenders seemed to gather strength from it, and the attackers to diminish.

"Why are they singing?" an aide asked, glancing at Kubodin.

Kubodin did not know. Facing death made people different. He knew that, but it was no good telling the aide. If he were unlucky, he would discover that himself soon enough.

He glanced around him, and saw what he was looking for. One of the men nearby carried a horn intended to be used to signal messages across the battlements. There were flags too, but it was the horn he was interested in. He unhooked the leather strap that held it over the man's shoulder, and put it to his mouth.

The sound that came from it was deep and somber, a fitting match to the song. He had little skill, yet still he managed to blend in with the voices, to rise to a high note when they did, and to blow a diminuendo when their voices fell away. Soon other horns sounded over the battlements, and the defenders raised their voices even louder.

As before, the heart went out of the enemy and they fled. This time though, the defenders did not jeer them. The song faltered, and the horns fell away. A silence descended, and all that could be heard was the moaning of the injured.

"That was the darndest thing I ever saw, or heard," Dakashul said.

The defenders were falling into a well-rehearsed routine now. Men came along the battlements with stretchers, retrieving the injured and dead. A hospital had been established below in one of the best buildings that had a roof that did not leak. After these came men with buckets of water and mops to clean up the gore. Then others threw down sawdust to dry the surface, for the defenders needed good footing to do their job.

Kubodin watched it all carefully, noting where improvements in efficiency could be made. He was still thinking about the fight that had just occurred though.

"Who among us would have believed just a short while ago," he said to Dakashul, "that so many tribes could fight together with such unity? For a moment there, there were no tribes at all. They were just Cheng."

Dakashul grunted. "True. I never thought to see that. But the Nagraks don't seem to have got the message."

"Give them time, my friend. Who knows? In ten years we might be sitting down drinking nahaz with them and discussing trade agreements."

The enemy retreat was inglorious, and it came on the back of past failure. That worried Kubodin, for it put pressure on the shamans and might force them to act. To that end, he watched closely to see what the shamans would do. His eyes failed him over the distance though, and the swirl of men made it hard to see as well.

He turned to the young aide closest to him. "Can you see the shamans or the chiefs? They'll likely be together at the rear of the army somewhere."

The young man shadowed his eyes with a hand and squinted.

"I'm not sure. I see a group on slightly higher ground at the back left that seem to be separate. There are riders going to it."

"That would be them," Kubodin replied. "The riders will be messengers giving details of the latest assault. Can you see anything of what's happening?"

The aide was silent a while, then straightened suddenly with wide eyes.

"They just killed one of the messengers! It must have been a chief who did it because a sword was used and not magic."

"Not good," Kubodin said. "Not good. They're worried, but there's nothing to be done about it."

Dakashul leaned a little over the battlement. "Maybe that's not the shamans. Look closer! See there, in the middle of the army? That looks like a large group of shamans coming through straight toward the gate of the fortress. The Nagraks are giving way to them."

Kubodin looked to where the chief pointed, and he saw what the Iron Dog had.

Dakashul stepped away from the battlement, and his hand dropped down to his sword hilt.

"Shar hasn't returned with help yet. If those shamans have decided to come at us with sorcery … we're doomed."

Kubodin felt his heart thud. "Have courage!" he answered. "To the gate! That's where they'll head."

He did not wait to see if anyone followed, but rushed down the tower steps toward the gate below.

4. Let Me Through!

Shar was not surprised. That the enemy had attacked Kubodin was a likely enough situation. The most important thing was that he had got the army into Chatchek Fortress. Getting in to help him was her problem.

"If we circle around and come down from the jagged hills behind, we can get in," she said. "The shamans cannot have blocked that route yet. It's very rough country, and no place for an army. If they've tried, Kubodin will be fighting them there to keep that way open as long as possible. That was a prearranged plan."

"Getting there will be difficult," Asana said. "There'll be scouts everywhere. We'll have to wait for nightfall to even have a chance."

Shar did not like to wait. Her army was there, fighting for her and the land. She should be with them.

Ravengrim approached. "There is another way," he offered.

"What way is that?" Shar asked, puzzled.

"Is not the quickest way in to go straight from here to the front gate?"

"It would be, except for the army. There are thousands there that would kill us in an instant."

Ravengrim nodded. "That would normally be true. Except the Nahat are shamans. We can walk through that army, and they would think we are of them. Why should they not? And you can walk in our midst, hidden."

Shar was dumbfounded. The boldness of the plan astonished her. Yet, it might just work. The more she thought about it the more likely that seemed.

The question that troubled her most was whether or not the Nahat could be trusted. If they were going to betray her though, they need not wait until they were in the midst of the army. This was already close enough.

"Do you really believe you can do this, and get us through?"

"I do."

Shar looked at her companions. They all seemed uncomfortable, but no one said no.

"Then we'll do as you say."

There was nothing to be done to prepare, at least as far as Shar could see. Yet the Fifty gathered together for a little while and talked in hushed tones. Quickly though, they seemed to arrive at an exact plan and then they gathered around Shar and her companions.

"Pull your hoods up," Ravengrim instructed. "And trust in us. We will get you into Chatchek."

Shar wished she felt as confident as he seemed, but there was nothing to do now but to proceed. It was a great risk, but so was trying to come up behind the fortress. Scouts might find them. Or getting there, they might still be barred from entry if the enemy had managed to infiltrate into the wild hills and steep cliffs that marched down to the rear of the fortress.

They stepped out of the woods that hid them, and the Nahat pulled up their hoods also. They did not walk normally anymore, but rather adopted a marching formation. From inside the phalanx, Shar could see little of what was going on. The enemy army was just a blur, seen here and there only between the few gaps the formation allowed.

She could sense confusion among them though. Or agitation. Then as the Nahat drew closer a strange sound drifted down from the distant battlements and over the flat lands where the enemy army was camped, and behind even them to roll faintly over the Fifty.

It was the sound of singing. And then horns.

"What in the world is that?" Huigar asked.

Shar had no idea. It was strange, and no one else seemed to know either. But battles brought out odd behavior in combatants at times.

"Whatever's going on, it's in Kubodin's favor," Asana said.

Shar peered through the gaps in the Fifty as best she could, and saw that the enemy were retreating from the walls.

They approached the rear of the army then, and word came back through the Nahat to be careful. Riders were approaching.

Those nearest Shar and her companions pressed in a little closer, and soon the thunder of hooves was heard. She guessed at a troupe of a hundred cavalry or so.

"Who are you and what do you want?" a voice boomed.

The Nahat came to a stop, and the voice of Ravengrim answered. He spoke quietly, but there was great authority in his tone.

"We are shamans, as any can see. And we come to put an end to this siege."

The leader of the riders hesitated. "You look like shamans. But you look different too."

"We are from Three Moon Mountain," Ravengrim replied. "Now let us pass. Time presses, and this siege must end before the day is done."

"Let it be so!" the rider cried, and a few moments later his troupe galloped off in a great rush.

The Fifty came to the very rear of the army then, and the soldiers, seeing they were let through by the cavalry, parted for them without question.

From what Shar could see as they walked into the very midst of the enemy was that the camp was in disarray. They had just been repulsed from the wall, and it did not look like it was for the first time. The men had a cast of fear to their faces, and fifty shamans passing close to them added to it.

They came to the center of the camp without difficulty. The strange singing from the fortress had ceased, and the soldiers here were quiet and subdued. Until one voice called out to them in challenge, and then hundreds of those near turned their attention on the Nahat.

"Who are you? Where do you go?"

Ravengrim answered as he had done before. "We are shamans, as you can plainly see. We come direct from Three Moon Mountain, and we will end this siege. Today."

There was a long pause. "I don't think you are," said the man. Shar caught a glimpse of him, and he seemed older. He was some sort of general, or maybe even a chief. Few others would dare to address a shaman so, even if he doubted who they were.

"Let me through," Ravengrim commanded, and there was such menace in his voice that Shar felt a shudder run through her.

"No."

"You dare to defy shamans? You will—"

The man cut him off. He seemed to be growing in confidence.

"I answer only to my own tribe's shamans, and I don't know who you are. Or if you are even shamans at all."

Ravengrim drew himself up. "Then I shall prove it, and your own shamans can reprimand you afterwards as you deserve."

The man held his ground, but those who were closest to him backed away slowly. Ravengrim lifted his hand and pointed a finger.

Nothing happened. Then the man began to tremble. It seemed as though a weight had settled over him, and his knees buckled. He straightened again, with great effort, his face turning red while his jaws clenched.

Ravengrim snapped his fingers, and the man fell suddenly to his knees. He cried out in pain, and then began to writhe.

Ravengrim looked around him. "Are there others here who question shamans' business?"

There was no answer save for the scuffle of dirt on the ground where the unfortunate man who had halted them continued to thrash.

"Then let us through or suffer."

Ravengrim waited on no answer, but strode ahead and the shamans followed him. Once more, the army parted, and like a ship splitting the waves the Fifty surged forward.

Shar felt sorry for the man Ravengrim had struck down. Of all the enemy, he was the one with the courage to do his job, and fate paid him for that with agony. The world was not just. Yet she caught a glimpse of him as she passed, and Ravengrim had relented. The man no longer seemed subject to whatever force of magic had afflicted him. He was trying to rise, but his legs were shaky.

The Nahat moved ahead, and now Ravengrim started to chant. His voice was deep and sonorous, and the language was Cheng, if full of strange words and inflections, which seemed fitting for shamans. It gave the impression that some magic was being worked, which was reinforced when the others joined in to emphasize certain phrases.

Yet still, they were in the middle of a horde of the enemy, and words alone might not continue to disguise them, still less protect them.

5. Reunited

At length, Shar could see the gate of Chatchek Fortress ahead. The last time she had seen it, the metal had been twisted and damaged by battle and time. Now it stood in its proper place, resplendent, and soldiers were behind it. Her soldiers. The soldiers of the Cheng Empire that could be.

Yet the gate barred her entry. She felt that keenly, and she might still die out here, torn apart by an entire army.

"Something is wrong," Huigar whispered in her ear.

"What?"

"Look to our rear right. There's a commotion there."

Shar had trouble seeing at first, for the Nahat did a good job of hiding her and her companions in the center of their formation. At times though, she caught a glimpse through the shifting group of the army beyond. It was still all around them, at least to the sides and the rear. Nothing seemed to stand between them and the gate. But there was turmoil to their right.

The gap closed for a few moments, and Shar could see nothing. Then it opened again, and wider as the Nahat began to walk faster. Whatever was wrong, they knew what it was better than she did.

That turmoil grew, and the faces of the enemy seemed confused. Then fearful. Shar soon saw why. A group of shamans emerged from the multitude. There were six of them, and they too seemed confused. Well they might be, for they must have heard rumor of this new group of shamans, and they must have doubted their veracity. If more of their kind were coming, they would have known about it. Yet the fifty did *look* like shamans, for they were, and that doubt confused them.

Confusion would only last momentarily though. At any instant they could order the entire army to attack.

Crossing that empty space between the army and the fortress seemed to Shar more dangerous than it had been in the midst of the enemy. Here, they could be seen by all. That included her own army too, and it might be that they would be attacked from both sides.

Shar was about to send word to Ravengrim that they must signal their friendliness to the fortress, when she saw that wise man had anticipated her. Hidden as best as possible from the shamans, he began to wave a cloth.

The Nahat broke into a run, and Shar and her companions were carried along with them. The shamans coming toward them cried out, and they too began to run. They were only a few hundred feet away now.

They came to the gate, and it was still barred against them. So far, they had not been attacked by the defenders. Confusion reigned among both sides. Shar pushed through the Nahat, and saw that Ravengrim was gesturing wildly, but that the soldiers on the other side were making no effort to open the gate.

Shar came up to them. There was no one there that she recognized. Swiftly she drew her two swords and held them high.

"It's Shar Fei!" she cried. "Let me in! Look into my eyes and you will see it's me!"

The soldiers at the gate stared at her, shocked, but from the shadows behind them a figure stirred and barked a command.

"Open the gate! Swiftly!"

Shar knew that voice, and few things had ever sounded so sweet to her than it did in that moment. The soldiers leaped to obey, and there was the heavy clang of metal as the great bars were removed that pinned the gate in place.

"Back a few paces!" Shar called out. She knew that as a defensive measure the gate would only open outward instead of inward.

They gave it room, and ponderously the gate swung toward them. A moment later, from behind, there was a flash of light. Shar turned to look, and saw that one of the Nahat had raised a shield of light. Against this, fire from the advancing shamans crashed.

From the high rampart, arrows rained down upon the shamans, and they retreated. Anger marred their faces, and she could feel their fury from here. It would be worse though if they knew she was among this group that had passed right through their army and into the fortress.

She hesitated a moment as the Fifty moved into the tunnel beyond the gate, then she went to the rear and showed herself, twin swords drawn, and a smile on her face.

"For the empire!" she cried out, and brandished the swords.

The shamans looked at her in shock, and then she was through the gate. It closed behind her with a boom, and they all hastened through the tunnel beneath the rampart and into the courtyard beyond.

Suddenly Kubodin was beside her, a roguish grin on his face. He took her into his arms and lifted her up.

"You're back! You did it!"

Shar laughed, and it seemed the first time she had done so in a long while.

"I did it, Kubi! I did it. Now let those shamans outside tremble!"

He put her down, but the smile did not leave his face. He glanced at Asana though, and then, surprisingly, he took the swordmaster into a hug as well.

Others were around them now, including a few chiefs.

"Spread the word," Shar told them. "Let all our army know that we have our own shamans from this moment forward. Shamans who serve the empire, and not themselves. Shamans who will defend them against sorcerous attack!"

A cheer went up among those gathered there, and word spread so that cheering was soon heard up on the battlements and from within the various buildings of the fortress.

The Fifty seemed a little taken aback at such a welcome. Evidently, they had not expected it and Shar wondered how they had been treated by Chen Fei's army.

She introduced Ravengrim to Kubodin, and they shook hands in the warrior's grip.

"If we may, we would like to rest now. Preferably in barracks of our own, if that is possible," Ravengrim asked. "We are little used to the company of others."

Kubodin bowed. "We have more than enough space for that, and you're welcome here. I'll arrange for some servants for you, and if you need anything, don't hesitate to ask."

"Before you go," Shar asked, "have you given thought to how you'll guard the ramparts against sorcery?"

"We have. Ten of us will be spread out on the battlements at all times. That is enough to deal with most things the enemy can cast against us. The remaining forty will be resting in our barracks, but will be swift to answer any call."

Kubodin had spoken briefly with a soldier, and that man led the Nahat away to wherever they were going to be billeted.

When they were out of sight, Kubodin whistled. "I bet that lot are going to put confidence in our army. Everyone feared what the shamans might do, but just like that," and he clicked his fingers, "we're going to feel a lot safer. For all the risk you took, Shar, it was worth it."

"I think so. But they're still only fifty. And there may be some things even they can't defend against."

She knew more of what shamans could do than most, and she knew also their numbers exceeded fifty many times over. This was not over yet, but Kubodin was right to feel a lot better about things.

There were many questions then on both sides about what had happened while they were apart. It took a good while to tell their stories, and during it Nahring reached them and hugged his daughter. Huigar held him tightly, and Shar felt bad. She had kept friend from friend and father and daughter apart. And though they did not know it yet, she would do so again. Perhaps with even greater risk that they would be separated forever.

"Let's go to the battlements," Shar said. "I want to study what the enemy is doing for a while."

They walked up the tower stairs, and Shar was pleased to see that the stonework was clean and in good repair. Almost, the fortress looked like it was only a decade old instead of built thousands of years ago.

At the top, she looked out over the mass of the enemy. She did not have much chance to study them though, for soldiers all along the top of the battlements called out to her and welcomed her back. Once more, she drew the Swords of Dawn and Dusk, and flourished them.

The swords brought a resounding cheer, and she sheathed them and then waved. Soon though, she turned back to study the enemy. It had not been wise to show them where she was, in case they attacked her with sorcery, but she had to acknowledge the people who fought for her.

"There are so many of them," Shar said softly.

"And yet you passed right through their middle," Kubodin replied. "They're not invincible nor infallible. We'll beat them Shar, we'll beat them."

Shar had a tour of the fortress after that, and everywhere she went soldiers greeted her with a cheer. So much, she thought, for the shamans' reward of ten thousand in gold on her head. Yet she watched everyone sharply, and Radatan and Huigar were always very close. It only took one lucky assassin … and she would be dead.

Kubodin had done a magnificent job of organizing things, and Shar could hardly believe that so much had been repaired in such a short time.

When she came to the wells, which were deep with plentiful water, she suggested more guards. Likewise with the buildings in which great quantities of grain and other foods were stored.

"Be wary of saboteurs," she told Kubodin. "One man with poison could kill more of us than a week's worth of fighting on the walls."

They went to the hospital next, and Shar spent a lot of time there. There were scores of wounded, some only lightly so, but others with grievous injuries that would ail them all the rest of their lives. If they survived at all.

She went among the patients, and sat on their beds as she spoke to them. They told her of their lives, and their families back at home, and she held their hand and listened. She missed hers as well, what she had of either.

At length, weary and subdued, Shar went to the room which had been prepared for her. It had a window, which was safe from assassins unless they could climb shear walls over fifty feet high, and at the front were a dozen guards.

Inside, she threw herself into a chair, and Kubodin ordered wine and food brought.

"What now?" he asked while they waited for their refreshments. "We hold Chatchek Fortress. We have the

Nahat, as you call them. But how do we progress the war? We cannot get new tribes to join us while we're stationary here."

Shar sighed, and felt weariness and anxiety flow through her in equal measure.

"No. But I have an idea. It wasn't just for defense alone, as important as that was, that I risked the quest for the Fifty."

6. He Is a Dead Man

Shulu studied the injured man she had been asked to heal. She knew what the shaman and the other witch-healer already knew. He was dying.

The other witch-healer seemed smug. She cared nothing for the man. All she was interested in was that her diagnosis was correct, and that Shulu would not show her up.

Beside her, the shaman was restless. He wanted to be elsewhere, but the injured man had likely cost him in training expenses, and if he died it would be a loss to the shaman.

Shulu studied the wounded man more closely. He looked as though he had been strong, but fever had wracked his body for days. There was a sword wound to his stomach, and it had become infected. That was clear the moment Shulu lifted the bandage. He was going to die, and already his mind was clouded with delirium. He was on the threshold to the other world, and he would pass before the day was done.

"Can you heal such as he?" the shaman asked.

Shulu sensed his impatience. He wanted the inevitable answer, and then he would dismiss her. He already had a witch-healer.

It was the other woman who answered. "He's a dead man. Nothing can save him now, and he will die ere nightfall."

Shulu gritted her teeth. The young man had heard that through his delirium, and she saw despair strike through to his heart deeper than the sword had pierced his flesh.

Her decision made, Shulu ignored both the other woman and the shaman. Instead, she reached out and took the man's hand in her own, and bent over to look into his eyes.

"You will live," she said. "I promise it. I have the skill to heal you, and I will. Endure, and wait."

The man gazed back at her, and there was a mixture of hope and skepticism in his eyes that was hard to watch. He wanted to believe, but he had heard the other's words.

Shulu retrieved some dry herbs from her pouch, and these she sprinkled under the bandage and then fixed it again.

She turned to the witch-healer, a middle-aged woman with a frown on her arrogant face.

"Will you make a tea with these please?"

The woman's frown deepened. "They'll not heal him. He's beyond herbs. I should know. I—"

"Be silent!" Shulu commanded. "Just do as you are asked."

The woman snatched the herbs and sniffed them suspiciously.

"What are these? I'll not give him something to drink unless I'm sure of their benefit."

Shulu smiled at her, but she knew no warmth reached her eyes.

"If you don't know what they are, you're not much of a healer. Now do as I say. The young man sickens while you talk rather than act."

The woman left the room in search of hot water and a cup, and Shulu was left alone with the shaman. She felt his gaze on her, and sensed his curiosity. She must be careful here. The herbs were useless in this case, at least to combat an infection, but they served as a subterfuge. She must not reveal her true power.

The purpose of the herbs was not to heal, but rather to put the injured man into a trance. From there, magic would do the rest. At least she hoped so. The man was on the brink of death. Every moment of delay made things harder.

She held the man's hand and whispered in his ear. She was not sure he could hear her though. Before, he had seemed somewhat lucid, but it had been transitory. Now he had sunk back into his fevered dreams, and she did not think he would wake again unless she healed him.

The shaman grew even more impatient, but said nothing. Shulu had made bold claims, and he was curious to see the outcome. If she failed though, he was likely entertaining himself by imagining some punishment for her.

The witch-healer returned, a cup in her hand. "It won't do any good. You'll see."

Shulu ignored her, and tested how hot the tea was. The woman was not incompetent, at least. It was merely warm and would not burn the man's mouth or throat.

It was not easy, and it took some time, but she managed to get the warrior to drink half of the contents. That was enough for her charade.

She began to chant. It was no more than a mumble, and the shaman would not hear her words. It was vital to conceal what she was doing from him, for the next part of the treatment, the true treatment, required magic that no simple witch-healer possessed. She made sure her back was turned to the others, and her head was bent low toward the patient.

Her spirit broke free from the shackles of the flesh, and merged into the mind of the dying warrior. In his fevered dreams he stood upon a craggy cliff. Below, was a great river roaring and crashing over rocks, but it was far, far below and the noise of the watery tumult was as a murmur.

"I must find the bridge. I must cross," the man muttered, looking for a way forward and not back at her.

He was already in the void, and to cross the river was to die.

"That river is death," Shulu replied. "Come. Speak to me. I will show you another way."

The man turned, surprised that someone was behind him. He stared at her for several moments.

"I know you. You are with the shaman and the witch-healer in my room." He frowned. "But that cannot be. I'm here."

Shulu stepped closer, but she never took her gaze away from his.

"You are in both places. Listen carefully, for I can help you. Here, you exist in the spirit. This is the void. This is the space between worlds. It is the gap between moments of time. All is here. Nothing is here. But back in the world you know, you are very sick."

The man studied her. "I am dead then," he said.

"Nearly so. Yet not quite. I was brought to you in time."

He stepped closer and peered at her. "You are no ordinary witch-healer."

"Perhaps not," Shulu replied. She wanted to change the subject, but he spoke again before she had a chance.

"I know who you are. I have seen your likeness in an old book, and that you are here, in the void, proves it. You are Shulu Gan. You are the grandmother who does not die. You are the Dragon of the Nation who guards the people."

The last was a term that Shulu had not head in a long time. Chen Fei had called her that, and it brought back to her good memories.

"I am she, but I do not go by that name, and names are not important here. Come, step closer. I will strengthen you and send your spirit back into your body. It is not your time to cross the river. Not yet."

The man approached, if hesitantly. Yet she saw that he still sensed the pull of the void. He wanted to cross the river, as all who came to this place were drawn to do. She must work quickly.

When he was close, he knelt before her. She lowered her hand to rest atop his head.

"Be still," she murmured. "Be at ease. I am with you. My strength is your strength. You will be well."

As she spoke she summoned her power. Magic coursed through her and into the warrior. He tensed. She sensed through him the pain that wracked his body. She found the infection, and her magic flowed from spirit to spirit and from spirit to body.

She sensed also, as though from a great distance, her own body. It was vital that the shaman not realize what she was doing, and that she had the magic to travel the void. She muttered inaudibly, and moved her head a little. It should be enough for him to think that she was merely offering up a prayer to the gods, and that if she healed the warrior she was favored by them.

Her concentration wavered. She felt the cold of the void slip into her bones, but the strength she had poured into the man had been enough. He stood now, and his face was not anxious and his eyes were bright.

"Great lady, you have saved me."

Even as he spoke, he began to fade as the pull of his body grew stronger and the call to cross the river reduced.

"Sleep, warrior of the Cheng Empire," she said softly. Even as he began to disappear, she let trickle forth a last tendril of magic. "Sleep. When you wake in your body, you will be refreshed. But of the void, and of me, you will forget."

The spirit of the warrior was gone, and she turned back and sought her own flesh. She hoped the last spell worked. If he revealed who she was, all her plans would be ruined. Even so, she did not regret healing him.

Shulu gave a slight start as she came back to her body. She checked the pulse of the warrior, and it beat steadily and strong. She wished she could say the same for herself, for the power she had used had been great.

She straightened and turned to the shaman. "He will live."

The shaman pursed his lips and raised an eyebrow. "He does seem ... more settled."

While they were talking, the witch-healer rested the back of her hand against the man's face.

"Well, of all the things. His fever is broken! I can't understand it."

"That," Shulu said carefully, "is because you don't understand the properties of herbs as I do."

The shaman had evidently arrived at a decision. "It seems, woman, that you're as good as you say you are. You may stay here, in my employment. I'm sure we can find a room for you."

Shulu curtsied. "That would suit me, sir. But there is the matter of wages."

"I'll give you standard wages, plus a room and food."

It was more than enough for Shulu. She had achieved her goal here, and would be able to spy to her and Shar's profit. But she must make things look real.

"Respectfully, sir, that will treat me the same as this other witch-healer, who has failed where I proved my skill. I ask for double her wage, and even that is a bargain. My skill will save you that amount tenfold every year."

The shaman narrowed his eyes coldly, and then laughed.

"Done! What you say is true."

Shulu curtsied again. She had won the respect of the shaman, but she had made a deadly enemy of the other witch-healer. If the woman would not be let go altogether, she at least would be shuffled to more menial tasks. And she would remember.

7. A Red Mist

It was a clear day, and bright. A cold breeze blew, but it was only faint. Shar enjoyed the touch of it against her skin.

The day was too beautiful for battle. Yet battle was about to begin. Men would die, and children would be orphaned. Those who lived would just have another terrible memory to add to others that would weigh them down all their lives. She knew that as well as any.

Nor could she even fight. She led the army again, and had for the last few days. The responsibility of command was hers, but she kept Kubodin close. He had been in charge, and he had done an excellent job. She wanted his experience at call, for he knew better than she how the soldiers reacted, and what had worked well for them, and not so well, while she had been away.

The little man tightened his rope belt. "It won't be long now."

He was right. A mass of the enemy came forward, but they stopped midway between their own army and the fortress.

"This is new," Kubodin said.

Shar wondered what they were doing, but then they began to chant. Instantly, she understood it was some design of the shamans. The Nahat had fooled the enemy by doing such a thing, and this was the reply of the shamans.

It was hard to pick out the words. It seemed to be a battle song, and it celebrated the great warriors of Cheng history.

"Ah," Shar said. "I've heard this before. Shulu sang it to me at times, but it was not remembered by the Fen Wolf Tribe."

She glanced at the member of the Nahat whose turn it was to stand with her on the tower.

"You would know this?" she asked.

"Of course, milady."

Shar started at that term of address. It was an honor, but it was not one she was used to hearing. It came deftly from the man though, as though it were a matter of course. And perhaps the term had more frequency in his era. Despite the fact that he seemed a tall, dark haired and young man, he had lived during the time of her famous forefather.

"Was it not sung," she struggled to recall his name from when they had met briefly several days ago, then it came to her, "Boldgrim, during the time of the emperor?"

"Of course. It was well known then. I'm surprised it is not now."

"Many things have been forgotten. They use it now as a Nagrak thing, I guess, little knowing its origin. I think they need an education on that. I believe some shamans have the ability to increase a person's voice so that it can be heard afar?"

"I have that talent, milady."

"Then let's put it to use."

It was a dangerous thing to do, but she leaped up to stand within the crenelation between two merlons on the rampart where the enemy would clearly see her. To misstep was to risk death, but she was careful, and she avoided looking down but rather gazed out over the mass of the enemy below and especially the group that had come forward and would soon attack.

"Hear me!" she cried out, and her voice boomed as though it were thunder across the fields.

As she spoke, she drew the Swords of Dawn and Dusk, and held them aloft. To her surprise, the sun caught the violet gems in the hilts and they flashed brightly. Then she realized, as that violet light surrounded her in a glowing nimbus, that Boldgrim was using magic to enhance the light even as he enhanced her voice.

"You know who I am. I am Shar Fei!"

The chanting below faltered in the face of her booming voice, and the soldiers knew she was addressing them directly, and they listened.

"Do you know that your Nagrak ancestors used to chant that same song? I know that you do. It has been handed down, generation to generation. But what was its origin?"

She paused, and allowed them to consider her words.

"I will tell you! Your ancestors chanted that same song, cried out those same words as they went into battle. And do you know who led them? It was Chen Fei! Your ancestors fought for him, and he made your lands the capital of the Cheng Empire. What you chant now for the shamans you once chanted for him!"

Again she paused, and when she resumed she spoke in a quieter voice, but it was filled with certainty.

"In the days ahead, you will sing that song for me, and it will not be to fight your Cheng brothers, but to honor the heroes who have fallen to fight off the yoke of the shamans."

She flourished the swords, then sheathed them and leaped back from the edge of the battlement. It had been a quick speech, but she did not want to give the shamans below a chance to contest the magic that Boldgrim had woven.

"Fine words," Kubodin said. "And true I hope, but it's not going to stop the attack."

That was true. Shar could see the shamans below barking orders and starting to drive the men forward.

"No, it won't. But it plants a seed of doubt in their minds, and that might grow in the future."

She glanced at Boldgrim, and nodded to him by way of thanks. He had done more than she asked, and he had done it well. She still had trouble accepting his age though, for neither his black hair nor his short black beard showed a sign of gray.

The enemy attacked them then. They came screaming and yelling, and a wave of fear came with them. Would they break through the defenses this time? Every soldier on the ramparts asked themselves that same question. Yet even in the time that Shar had been here, she noticed that the confidence of the defenders was growing. They were getting used to the idea of fighting behind a wall, and they liked it. Better still, they began to feel that they could hold it as long as food remained. And they had built up a good store of that, and more was still arriving via the mountainous tracks behind the fortress.

For all the fury of the Nagrak attack, it faltered swiftly. The heart had gone out of them even as the first few died atop the walls, and despite the haranguing of shamans, they rolled back even as the sea pounds into a cliff and then subsides, spent.

They watched from the tower, and Shar felt the confidence of her army grow even more.

"I see Asana down there," Kubodin said. "I'm going for a walk on the ramparts to talk to him and the men."

Shar watched him go, and signaled Radatan and Huigar to go with him. She did not like to keep them constantly by her side, prisoners of their duty, especially when danger had passed.

Kubodin had changed since they had first met, even if he looked the same. Responsibility had brought his true self to the surface.

She did not really like Asana fighting on the wall. She could not afford to lose him, and it would devastate her if he died, but in truth there was little risk. His skill was sublime, and in a cold sort of way this was practice for him. One did not become the best without fighting in real battles. Or stay the best merely by swishing a sword through the air in pretty prearranged forms.

Nor could she deny his influence over the men. He spread himself out, fighting in a different place every time the enemy attacked, and all those men fought beside him with pride and tried to live up to his high standards. If they lived, they would one day tell their grandchildren that they had fought beside the legendary Asana Gan.

Even as she watched though, something strange began to happen. The battlement had blood on it from where, here and there, a handful of soldiers had broken through. They had been quickly slain, and now buckets of water were being thrown over the patches before sawdust would be laid down. Yet as the water and blood mingled, a red mist rose.

Shar had never seen anything like it. She did not know what it was, but even as she began to be alarmed, that mist took the form of a dozen men, red wraiths with crimson swords, and they streaked up straight toward her through the very air.

It was the work of shamans, and Shar drew her swords and felt them pulse with magic in her hands. The attackers arrowed for her, but the two aides who were with her were in the way. These were killed swiftly, the crimson swords slicing through them, and then the wraiths came for their true target.

Shar had just enough time to back away so that a wall protected her from behind, and the wraiths could not get at her from all sides. Yet they drove at her, swords flashing and a leer on their mist-like faces that seemed like corpses under water.

Each time her swords met a crimson blade, there was a flash of sparks that fell to the stone flagging like embers. Two she slew, if such creatures lived. And they screamed as they died, which she took to mean that the spirit of the shaman inside the magic had been injured or even killed. She could not stand against so many though, and even if help were coming from the soldiers on the rampart immediately below the tower, they would not arrive in time.

There was a flash of light then, bright and violet. A slow rumble as of thunder followed it, and it seemed that the foundations of the tower shook.

"Milady!" The cry came to her ears, and though her eyes were dazzled, she yet saw that a path had been cleared through the wraiths to her right side. There Boldgrim stood, his staff held high and magic wreathing him as though he wore a mantel of light.

She darted through that gap. What had happened to the wraiths there, she did not know. They had been blasted by sorcery out of existence so far as she could see. But there were still others that might kill her.

They rushed for her as she sped through the gap. The closest fell to a sweep of her sword, the red mist spraying in all directions and evaporating. Then she was by Boldgrim's side, and there, the two of them against the many, they fought together.

Her swords claimed another wraith, and then light flared again from Boldgrim's staff, spraying violet fire from its tip. The wraiths rushed at them, their unearthly cloaks billowing behind them and their eyes alight with the fever of battle.

Shar felt that fever too. The shamans had conjured sorcery to kill her, and anger rose in response. The Swords of Dawn and Dusk spun in deadly arcs, and more wraiths died.

They were diminished now to two, but before Shar and Boldgrim could attack them, the magic dissolved and the wraiths vanished. The shamans who controlled them had given up.

The smell of blood was in the air, and the walls were crimson. Some dark spell of blood magic had been used, but once more she had survived. This time, thanks to Boldgrim.

"You stood by me," she panted. "I'll not forget it."

The man bowed. "I did not serve the emperor well. I hope to make it up with you."

Others arrived then, swords drawn, and horror on their faces. They had nearly lost their leader.

"I'm sorry," Kubodin said. "I should not have left your side."

Radatan and Huigar laid down their swords. "We are not worthy to be your bodyguards," Huigar said, and there was the sheen of tears in her eyes.

"Pick those swords up," Shar commanded. "You are the best of the best, and the most trusted by me. Who could have known the shamans were going to attack me at just that moment?"

"We should have guessed that they had been waiting for such a situation," Kubodin said.

"None of you are to blame," Shar answered. "Now, enough of this. We have more important things to do."

An idea had occurred to her. She had revealed herself to the enemy when she entered the fortress, and she had done that to annoy them. It was a little thing, but it no doubt had an effect. This attack just now might be a response to it. But it was important to show that it had failed. They would know that already, for the shamans had been here on the battlements, but the enemy army had seen it unfold, and their eyes would be on her. There was something she could do to show her disdain for the shamans and their use of sorcery against a warrior, and to portray a lack of concern at anything they or their army could do. It was another tactic designed to annoy them, to dishearten them, and to sap their morale.

She gave swift orders for the blood to be washed from the walls, and for certain things to be brought to the top of the tower. It surprised all those around her, but she merely grinned. Showmanship was one of the great skills any general must possess.

The enemy below seemed uneasy. The men on the walls were joyous, for they had thrown back another attack, and their leader, with the help of a member of the Nahat that she had gone to so much trouble to bring to the army, had fought magic with magic, and won.

Shar turned her mind to Boldgrim. He had probably saved her life, and done it at great risk to his own. He could have hung back and waited a few moments, and then claimed afterward that he was only one against many shamans, and that he could not save her.

She did not quite trust the Nahat yet. But Boldgrim, she now trusted with her life. He had proven his loyalty. She approached him where he stood on the edge of the rampart, gazing out at the lands all around.

"Thank you, again," she said.

He flicked his dark-eyed gaze to her. However young he seemed, those eyes told a different story.

"I just did what I'm here for, milady. It was nothing special."

There was a certain truth to that. On the walls, men risked their life daily, and would keep doing so for the foreseeable future. None of them had his powers though.

"It was special to *me*," she replied. "I have Radatan and Huigar as bodyguards, and I trust them with my life. They cannot defend against sorcery like you can, though. So, I offer you the same trust, if you accept it. Will you take on more than just serving as a Nahat? Will you become one of my bodyguards, and help protect me against magic as Radatan and Huigar help protect me against steel?"

Boldgrim seemed surprised, and a shadow of doubt crept over his face. She did not know how he felt about once serving her forefather. He had hinted that he had not served the emperor well. Perhaps there was more there than just the general betrayal by the Nahat. If so, he might share it in time.

He bowed slightly, and then once again his face was an inscrutable mask, that veil that shamans, and some chiefs, could draw over the features to hide their thoughts.

"Yes," he replied. "Of old, the guards who protected the emperor were held in the highest honor across the land. I will serve you, and try to live up to that."

Soon after, Shar's plan was set in motion. A table and chairs were carried up the tower stairs, and they were placed right on the edge of the rampart A white cloth was laid over the table, and a morning tea served. Shar sat down and invited several others to join her. There they ate and drank and laughed. And all the while the eyes of the enemy were upon them.

It was a childish thing to do. Perhaps. But it was deadly serious too. It would show the shamans that she had disdain for them. It would show the Nagrak soldiers that she was calm and at peace. While they spilled their blood to try to take a fortress that was near-impossible to take, their opponents celebrated.

It was an affront to the enemy. It might flare their hatred and spur them to greater actions. That was a risk. She did not think that would be the outcome though. The soldiers would feel dejected. It would drain their morale.

So too the shamans. For them though, and the chiefs among the enemy, it might force them into some hasty decision. The more she annoyed them, the less rational they would be. That would work to her advantage. So she hoped, anyway.

8. Stalemate

The days passed, as they always did. There was at least one attack, which was repulsed. Sometimes, there were several. It seemed to the defenders that this had always been their life, and all else was but the shadow of distant memory.

It was a routine that gave Shar ample time to think. She already knew what she must risk next, but she weighed up the decision in her mind, over and over again. She looked for a different way. There was none. She looked for a path that entailed less risk. There was none. She looked for a choice that offered better hope of a united Cheng Empire. There was none.

This day had been different from the others. It dawned to the slow rumble of thunder in the distance. It was not the time of year for storms, but the weather recked nothing for the battles of men. In the fortress, they were protected from the worst of it. When the rain came, there was a minimum number of soldiers exposed on the ramparts. They endured it in the knowledge that when their shift was done, they would be indoors again and out of the wet and cold.

The Nagrak horde below huddled miserably, unable to light fires to keep themselves warm, or to cook with when the midday hour arrived. This would be bad for them, but in the days to follow the full effects would be seen. Some of them would become sick, and then that sickness would spread.

Shar spent an hour on the tower above the gate. She favored the right one over the left. It was where Boldgrim had saved her, and she knew the enemy looked for her there. That she yet lived must irk them, and that gave her pleasure.

It was there that she made her final decision, amid the whipping wind and driving rain. In the distance, lightning flashed, but fortunately the storm rode the western horizon and did not get near enough to be a threat at Chatchek. If it did, it would be hard to keep soldiers on the high walls. It would be much harder for the Nagraks though, so she almost wished for it.

Her decision taken, she made arrangements for a meeting. She stayed on the tower, amid the gloom and distant flashes of light, until word reached her that all those who were invited had been notified.

With a final look at the subdued enemy, she left the tower.

Kubodin had told her of a place, deep down in the main keep, which was perfect for meetings. Secret meetings, anyway. She had no wish to be overheard, and her plan revealed. Only those who were absolutely necessary had been invited, and they were all being led to this basement room separately. Most of them did not even know it was there themselves.

She passed into the keep, and wandered some of its dark passages with only her three bodyguards. When no one was looking, she opened a rarely used door, and closed it behind them. They went through a dark corridor, and found the concealed door at its end. Then, they followed a spiral staircase that led deep into the foundations of the keep.

It was dark and damp, but there were torches there that someone had lit and fixed to sconces on the wall. That would have been Kubodin's doing. Then there was another corridor, and another flight of stairs.

At length, they came to a corridor and saw several guards standing outside a large door constructed of oak slabs and bound by thick strips of iron. It was hard to say what this room had been used for in the ancient past, but it served her purposes well today.

The guards let them in without a word being spoken. They were Two Raven men, and handpicked by Kubodin.

She was the last to arrive, and the others were waiting for her, seated around a large trestle table that had been hastily built here out of old doors. There were several wine bags on the table, and a collection of goblets.

Only the chiefs of the tribes were inside, and Asana who was always accepted as one of their number. And now her and her guards. The less that heard this discussion, the better. It would reduce the chances of the enemy discovering a plan that would shock them, and might begin to turn the war against them.

Shar took a seat that had been left for her at the head of the table. Her guards stood behind her.

"You will be wondering why I called this strange meeting," she began.

"It doesn't seem quite normal," Targesha replied. "But I wouldn't know."

He was the new chief of the Green Hornet Clan, appointed by Shar on the day of the funeral of the old one. He would not know what was normal for these sort of meetings, but he was right to detect that this was different.

"Forgive the precautions. Our army is large now, and the enemy will have placed spies among us. What we decide in this room is going to be important, and the fewer who know the better."

Kubodin leaned back in his chair. "Then let's get to it. I have a feeling we're not going to like it, but that we'll agree in the end."

He smiled as he spoke, and some of the chiefs laughed. But that humor did not reach Kubodin's eyes. He knew her well, and he guessed that she would not go to so much trouble to keep a meeting secret unless she had a bold plan. And bold plans were dangerous.

"Well," Shar said, "let me state the obvious first. We command Chatchek Fortress, and that has proven a great advantage. The enemy hurl themselves against the walls and are thrown back in defeat each time. We can hold out here for a year or more, and they cannot defeat us unless they use magic."

Dakashul leaned forward, his stocky arms crossed on the table.

"What of the Fifty?" he asked. "Aren't they our protection against magic?"

"Of course. But a year is a long time. Should they choose, our enemy could gather a hundred shamans. Or two hundred. Or more. Maybe even the ones that are here could invoke a magic difficult to counter. Magic is uncertain and unpredictable, both in defense and attack."

There was a general mutter of approval at that. Apart from Boldgrim, these men were warriors who trusted in steel and their own skill. They did not really like magic, though they much preferred it when there was some on their side.

"What all this means is that we're at a stalemate. Unless something unexpected happens, this siege might go on for a very long time."

Asana glanced at her, his gaze quick and intelligent, with a hint of curiosity.

"You need more than a stalemate," he said. "You need an advantage."

"Exactly so. I can't progress the war against the shamans from here. I can only hold the Nagraks at bay. What I need. What the Cheng Empire needs, if there's to be one, is for rebellions to break out in other places."

Argash looked earnestly at her. "That would be good, if it were to happen. Not only would it bring more tribes to our cause, but it would make the shamans send an army elsewhere. That would be less for us to fight. But I can't see other tribes joining us at the moment. Winter is coming on, and most chiefs would rather see how you fare in *this* battle, your first major conflict. Win, and a lot will come to your side in spring. But how can you win? We cannot venture beyond the walls of Chatchek. They outnumber us by too many."

"Precisely, Argash." Shar looked around the room. It was dimly lit, for there were no windows, and the light from the torches was fitful. She could see the curiosity on all their faces though.

"A stalemate is defeat to us," she continued. "It's nearly impossible for us to win, as things stand. It's equally hard for the enemy to win while the walls of Chatchek protect us, but that situation cannot go on forever. I have a plan to change all that. There's a way to reach the other tribes, to convince them to rebel, and to start a war against the shamans from a second front."

She paused again. So far, so good. Her plan sounded grand. At least the idea of starting that second front up against the enemy. They would not like the means though.

Dakashul frowned. "You've already sent messages to all the tribes. It would be hard to send more out from here, and even if you did what could they do that the previous ones couldn't?"

"Good points, Dakashul," Shar said. "Except there's one messenger who can better convince them than anyone else."

"Who?"

"Me. When they see my swords, and look into my eyes, they'll *know* I'm the heir to Chen Fei. I won't be a rumor then. I'll be flesh and blood. I'll stir them into action as I have done with all of your tribes. Time was, when I was by myself. Then I gained the support of Asana and

Kubodin. Then tribe after tribe." She swept an arm out to encompass them all. "I'll start a fire in the west of the Cheng lands that will rage toward us, and we toward it. The enemy will be caught between."

Asana was not swayed by her dramatic explanation. As always, he went straight to the heart of the matter.

"How will you get there, though? The fortress is cut off, except for the rear. But those mountain trails won't stay open for long, and they must already be dangerous. The scouts of the enemy will be all through there."

"There is a way," Shar said. She could not quite bring herself to say it. Going to Nathradin had been a step too far, and she had determined not to take such risks again. But for the Cheng people, there was no risk she would not take. It was better to die than suffer the corrupt rule of the shamans.

The chiefs looked at her, curious but doubtful. They could see no way. And even if she could escape the net around Chatchek, to reach the other side of the Fields of Rah and contact the tribes beyond the Nagraks was a journey of around five hundred miles. It would be undertaken during winter too, which might turn a month's journey into two months. Assuming she was not killed along the way, by enemies or weather.

She eased back in her chair and glanced over her shoulder at Boldgrim.

"Shulu told me there was a way to travel. A way that was not ordinary. The shamans learned the magic of it from Malach Gan in days of old. At least, the Nahat learned it from him, for it was a lòhren magic from elsewhere in Alithoras, and he was both lòhren and shaman. It was kept secret from the other shamans, was it not?"

Boldgrim gazed at her, and he tried to stammer out an answer, but no words came. His face turned pale, and then he regained his composure. Except for his eyes. There was fear in them such as she had not even seen when fighting the attack of the wraiths.

9. The Mach Furr

"Come," Shar said. "There *is* such a way to travel, is there not, Boldgrim?"

The man had shown fear, and he was not the sort to do so except in rare circumstances. He did not show it now, but there was a reluctance in his voice when he answered.

"There is. It's called the Mach Furr."

Shar pressed ahead. "And by using this magic, I can travel where I wish, and swiftly?"

"Of course, milady. No one has used that magic for a thousand years though. Not in Cheng lands, anyway. And even in the past it was not used except in desperate need."

Shar knew all this. The name of Mach Furr was new to her though. Shulu had not told her that.

To Shar's surprise, it was Asana who revealed knowledge of the magic that he should not have.

"I have heard tell of this Traveling," he told them. "It's said to be dangerous, and even lòhrens shun the use of it. When they do risk its use, they have artifacts, or portals such as a ring of standing stones, that aid them. Is there such a thing here, in or near Chatchek?"

Boldgrim gave the swordmaster a peculiar look, as though he were suddenly looking at him properly for the first time. The Nahat, it seemed, did not think highly of warriors, but knowledge of magic in those who should not have possessed it certainly got their attention.

"It is as you say. Only worse in our lands, for no such portals were ever built. We must create a gateway ourselves, and that makes it doubly dangerous. Do you know where that gateway leads?"

Asana tilted his head sideways, as though trying to remember something. Kubodin, to everyone's surprise, gave the answer.

"The magic makes use of the void. The living bodies of those who Travel pass through the world of spirit, and that's a dangerous place to be."

Shar realized that she should not be surprised at anything Asana or Kubodin knew. They had been to foreign lands together, and had stayed there for many years. She did not think that time had been uneventful, though they did not speak of their adventures. Undoubtedly, much had happened.

Boldgrim replied. "You call it dangerous for a living body to travel through the void, but it is peril such as few can comprehend. The ways of Mach Furr are perilous beyond speaking. One mistake is death, and to die there is not just to risk death itself, but to risk the destruction of your very soul."

Shar knew as much. "I will risk it," she said. "I must, for to stay as we are is, ultimately, to lose. Even if it takes a year or longer, the shamans will rally other tribes together and build their numbers. At some point, despite the walls that give us an advantage, they'll overrun us. Even if they don't, sooner or later our supplies will give out, and you can be sure they're already looking at ways to choke off the materials we still receive through the mountain pathways behind us. And if not those things, then the shamans themselves will mass in numbers great enough to overcome the Fifty. So, it's already a given that I must go, the question is this. Will you, or another of the Nahat, invoke this magic?"

She turned to Boldgrim as she spoke, and once more she saw that flicker of fear.

Yet he overcame it. "I know the magic. I will guide you through the void, but if we come out the other side and reach our destination, I will be surprised."

It was not a promising situation. Much was to be gained though. It could win them the war, but the chiefs did not like the risks to her. If she were killed, that would lose them the war, and their lives with it. The shamans would set an example of them for future generations.

They did not object though.

Kubodin, who obviously knew more than most of them here the dangers of traveling the void, spoke up.

"Let me come with you, this time."

"I cannot." It broke Shar's heart to say that. She wanted him with her, but he was the best to lead the army in her absence. He had done well last time, and the men and the chiefs trusted him. To place a new chief at the head of them all was to risk problems. "You know the reasons why as well as I do."

He gave no answer, but bowed his head.

"Then you're stuck with my company again," Asana said.

"And mine," both Radatan and Huigar said at the same time.

She accepted their offer with a sad smile. She was risking their lives. More, she was risking their souls.

"What guard will you take with you?" Argash asked. "Fifty? A hundred men? You don't know how these other tribes will receive you."

Shulu had told her of the limitations of this great magic, but Boldgrim answered before she could.

"Five is as many as I can manage. I have to open a gateway ... it takes enormous power and will not last long. A few seconds at most."

Kubodin shook his head, and looked at Shar. "You take such great risks. No one will really appreciate it ten years after you win this war."

That might be true. But the people she knew and loved, and Kubodin was one of them, would appreciate what she did. Always.

"When do we leave?" Asana asked.

10. So Be It

It was cool atop the pagoda. Outside, the early morning sun was bright, but beneath the highest eave of the tower it was still in shadow.

Olekhai sipped melon juice out of a crystal glass. It was likely the last of the season, for the fall melons had all been harvested and it was now too cold for anything to ripen. Winter was coming. The year was dying, and with it, likely, this age of men.

He would not be sorry. Too long he had lived, and too many cycles of summer and winter had he seen. Immortality was striven for, yet Shulu knew better. No greater curse could there be.

The melon juice tasted of ash. He remembered what sweetness was though, and that made it all the more unpalatable. There was nothing to be done, however. He must eat and drink. Depriving himself of sustenance made him weak, but did not kill him. He knew because he had tried.

Nor did a blade end his life, either. All it brought was pain, and even the healing was uncomfortable. Once, he craved immortality. Now that he had it, he wanted to be rid of it. Such was the lot of humanity. They were never happy.

This morning he was close to it though. His plots were working, at least so far as he could see. Right now, what unfolded below in a part of the training grounds of the Ahat was of more interest.

The land was flat, and there was a clear area of grass below the tower, and a ring of forest beyond. A sport was being played out down there, and he watched intently.

Few things gave him pleasure anymore. This was one, and his eyes gleamed with anticipation. The combatants had stalked each other through the trees for some while. They were close to each other now, but did they know it?

From Olekhai's high vantage, he could see much that they could not. One lay concealed beneath a shrub, dagger in hand. His hood was pulled up, and he remained motionless. Only the fact that Olekhai had seen him find and utilize the hiding place enabled him to observe him. Otherwise he was perfectly hidden.

The other man evidently did not see him. He stalked along the path, taking only a step every once in a while. For the rest of the time, he remained still and listened. But he headed on a route that would very soon take him within a few feet of the one who lay in wait.

Olekhai leaned forward, and his breath came more quickly. The game was nearly played out, and soon the stalking man would die, and the other would be raised up to a position of leadership in the Ahat. So were all such positions in the Ahat gained, for only the strong were needed. The weak were useless. Such was the rule of nature, and Olekhai, like the ancients he had studied in his youth, followed the way of nature. The way of humanity was flawed.

The stalker began to step, and then paused mid stride. Somewhere in the trees, not far from him, a white-headed sparrow began to call, and others joined in.

It was not a threat though, and the stalker resumed his slow advance. The sudden noise must have surprised and frightened him momentarily. He moved more slowly now, then paused once more.

Olekhai was growing impatient. It was time this game ended. The next step or two would see the man unwittingly enter within range of his opponent, and then it would all be over. Olekhai urged him on with his thoughts.

It seemed to take forever, and then the man stepped forward. One pace. Two paces. Then the trap was sprung.

From beneath the shrubbery the hidden ambusher leapt up, dagger glinting in the morning light. Yet he was surprised himself, and so was Olekhai.

The stalker had a knife hidden up his sleeve, and his arm snaked out in a flinging motion even as his attacker began to move. The hunter had been the hunted, and all along the man stalking had known his ambusher was there, and played into the trap in order to get close enough to strike.

The knife arced through the air, and it struck the man in the shoulder. It was not a killing injury, but it would cause great pain and hinder his movements.

So it proved. He tried to jump back out of the way, but his movement seemed sluggish. The stalker was on him, and several blows were thrown in quick succession.

Olekhai could hear the grunts of pain, as the man cried out. But he was not defeated yet. He dropped low, and drove in at the other man's legs tackling him to the ground.

The pair rolled, vying for a strong grip or to bring their knives to bear. The stalker had drawn a second one now, and already they both bled from several wounds. As far as Olekhai could see, they were all superficial though. The stalker, a taller man and thin, was less suited to grappling than the other man who was stockier. He managed to get away and come to his feet.

The two combatants faced each other. They made no sound now, and they both held knives deftly before them.

It was the only type of weapon they were allowed to carry for this contest, except for the knotted cord they could use for choking.

Olekhai was impressed. The stalker had set a trap that took courage and involved great risk. He had almost won, too. But his execution had not quite been perfect. So now he faced an opponent, if wounded, who might still best him.

The two burst into a sudden surge of attacks, defense and counterattacks. More blood was drawn, but still no decisive victory was obtained.

Around them, the forest was silent, and the sparrows had either flown away or else penetrated deep into some bush in alarm. The two combatants separated. For all the flurry of their activity it seemed it was mostly feints and maneuvering to try to find an opening, for there seemed to be no new injuries.

The stalker appeared unsteady on his legs, but then he quickly straightened and flung his knife at his opponent. It was another bold move, for each combatant was only allowed two knives. If this failed, he would have lost both weapons.

It did fail. The other man leaped to the side and ducked, the blade arcing past him into the shrubbery. But the stalker was already moving, and he leaped also, driving forward with a double-footed kick that struck his opponent full in the chest.

The two rolled and struggled on the ground. Olekhai could not see clearly now, and he was not sure who was who. Then one of them was on top, his arms pulling back. It could not be seen from the pagoda, but doubtless he held his chole-cord in his hands and was putting it to use.

The man beneath struggled violently. Olekhai breathed hard. A long while seemed to pass, and all movement stopped. Still the man on top kept the cord tight, and then at last he stood, contemplated the corpse a moment, and retrieved his knives. It was the stalker who had won, and perhaps there was a lesson in that. Things were not always as they seemed, and Olekhai wondered if there was something in that which applied to his own circumstances.

The winner of the contest walked over the level training field directly beneath the pagoda, and there he paused and bowed, offering his respects.

Olekhai stood, and saluted him. The man had been a surprise, but he had won in the end. More assassins were needed like him. Men who had courage and boldness, and who did not always strike from the hidden shadows.

Servants came out of the tower and took the combatant away to a place where his wounds would be tended. The corpse was removed as well, and it would be buried in an unmarked grave.

The melon juice was finished now. Olekhai wished for more, but there was no point. There never was. The taste of it was nothing but a bitter reminder of all that he had lost.

His thoughts turned to Shulu. It was she who had cast such a despicable curse upon him. Not even the gods knew its origins. Or if they did, the ones he had dealt with claimed otherwise.

Shulu was dead though. The tagayah must have seen to that by now. It had been another gift of the gods, or at least some of them. They wanted her dead, and with her Shar. There had been no confirmation though, and that troubled him. He would have liked to have seen Shulu die himself. First, for the deep pleasure of it. Second for the certainty.

Not all things could be his though. And the gods were capricious. They favored him at times, or at least those he knew, but at other times they were aloof and disdained to give him help.

It was a strange deal he had struck though, and with just one god and not the others. He did not care about the consequences, but naturally he was curious. What benefit would it be to a god to take on the fleshly form of a human and rule as an emperor?

There could only be one real answer. Ambition. What could stand in the way of a god-king with a massive army? Not very much. First, neighboring lands would fall, and then those armies that were conquered would be joined to the empire's. So it would continue until all Alithoras was one thralldom.

Olekhai enjoyed the irony. Shar wished for the old days of empire, and the shamans fought against her. But in her winning of it, she would lose. He would control her. And then the god, whom the shamans worshipped, would take her place and create an even larger empire. One the shamans would serve, or be made to serve by force. In place of the emperor that they would hate would be a god-king they loved.

None of it was his concern though, and Olekhai brooded patiently, waiting for the next step, and planning the ones after. All he wanted was death. The curse upon him was terrible, and life everlasting without love, or joy, or the ability to satiate desire was a far greater punishment than anything he had deserved. What was the death of an emperor in the greater scheme of things?

All he wanted was death. He wondered about that. It had been his goal for centuries, and yet when Shar sat upon the throne of the Cheng Empire, and his curse was lifted, would he feel the same way?

Perhaps he would.

He could not imagine feeling otherwise now. Yet once he had been ambitious too. Might not he find a role at the right hand of the god, and exercise power greater than even Chen Fei had?

It was something to think on.

11. A Tear in Reality

Boldgrim was surprised at the reaction of the Nahat when he told them of Shar's plan, and his intention to help.

Some had outright called it madness. He did not entirely disagree. That had been his first reaction. Yet the need for such a step was compelling. If it worked, it would save lives. Without it, the rebel army would be slowly crushed, and thousands would die. Or, less likely as far as he could see but still possible, the shaman army would be slowly crushed. In any event, the outcome would be the same. A tragic loss of life.

If Shar were successful, she could tilt the balance so far in her favor that the shamans would admit defeat. And if they did not, the tribes themselves might all swing to her side, and then it would not matter what the shamans thought.

Others of the Nahat had reacted differently though. Always they had been a sect that pursued knowledge. That was what differentiated them from the shamans who sought power. And to travel the Mach Furr, which few had ever done, was an adventure from which much could be learned. Assuming he came back alive to report what happened.

Most were just unprepared for the proposal, and he saw them still trying to come to grips with the plan.

Having their own barracks had been a good idea, and they could discuss such things in private. And even those who were presently guarding the rampart still participated. They communed mentally with those in the barracks, a trick he did not think the shamans of this time had perfected.

"I think it too dangerous," Ravengrim said. "I want Shar to succeed, and this might well be a great step forward in that direction, but she cannot beat the shamans if she's dead."

So the debate continued in the dull barracks. The window shutters were closed in order that they may not be heard, and the only real light came from the hearth used to cook food. A log burned in it, and though the chimney had been cleaned it did not function quite properly and smoke drifted back into the room at times instead of being drawn out.

There were other points of view. Some said the knowledge gained of Mach Furr would be invaluable. The Nahat must think not just of the present but the future of the Cheng nation. Who knew in what ways such knowledge might be used to benefit the people in the future? Especially in war, for while the Cheng fought among themselves now, at some time ahead as had been in the case in the past, other nations might seek to invade.

Boldgrim had listened to the arguments, and both the yes and no sides were correct. Yet Shar had asked him to do this thing, and looking into her eyes he had been unable to refuse. There was something about her. It was more than violet eyes. There was some aspect to her character, her own willingness to sacrifice her life for her country, which drew the same feeling out of others.

"We could debate all day," he said. Certainly, they had in the past. It was in their nature to interrogate a topic until all definite answers could be gained from it, and when that was done to keep going until they deduced more, and then to make predictions based off deductions. "Yet ultimately the decision is mine, is it not?"

To this Ravengrim and the other elders assented, and the rest of the Nahat also, even those on the walls adding their approval.

"Then I will go. I am the youngest of the Nahat, and the one that can be spared most. If I am lost, even my immortal spirit, then it is the least loss to our cause."

"*Not* the least," answered Ravengrim, though he would not, or could not, expand on that comment when pressed.

Shar stood with Asana on the wall. They had toured the battlement, talking with the men and encouraging them. Shar told them all, freely and without deception, that she was going on another quest. One that might win the war. She avoided answering exactly what it was though. *Wait and see*, she had said. *You'll like my plan as you've come to like my previous ones.*

She knew that was true. But she had not told them of the risk. In truth, she was tired of such risks. Sooner or later her luck would run out, but if she did not take such chances she could not hope to defeat the shamans, a force more powerful than she.

"Where will you go?" Asana asked.

Shar looked quietly around her to make sure no one could hear the answer. Even her bodyguards were not close enough just now.

"To the Nahlim Forest," she answered. "It's the farthest west of all Cheng lands, but populous. If I can rouse those tribes, then we can drive in at the enemy from two sides."

"I've been there," Asana said quietly. There was something in his tone that drew Shar's attention. He had never said where he had been born, or what his tribe was. There were stories of course, but no two of them gave the same answer. It might be that the Nahlim Forest was home to him. Maybe. She would not ask him though. Part of those legends also said his childhood was unhappy, as he was teased and bullied for not being pure Cheng. She would not bring such memories back to him if she could help it.

"Do you think the forest tribes will join you?" he asked.

It was a subject to which she had given much thought. Nothing was conclusive though.

"Of old, those lands were great supporters of Chen Fei. I hope, and I think, they'll be favorable to me. Circumstances drove me eastward into the Wahlum Hills when this began, but I always had it in mind to go to the Nahlim Forest first, thinking those tribes would be my best allies."

"It could be," Asana said, "that they'll prove so. You might find that even a thousand years later they still love the old emperor. But that's a nostalgic love of things gone by in their history. The threat and the power of the shamans over them today is real and recent. It will dominate. To win them over, you'll need to be at your best."

It was good advice. Shulu had always said much the same thing. The loyalty of no tribe was a given. Nor was the enmity of a tribe. The past was in the past, and she must give them hope and confidence in the future if she were to win support.

Their conversation turned to a slightly different matter then. Asana showed a detailed knowledge of the area, listing the many tribes of the forest and surrounding lands. Shulu had tutored her in all this, but it was good to get a different perspective on it. And one that might be more recent. Shulu's knowledge had mostly been up-to-date, thanks to the vast array of spies in the land that reported to her. Yet sometimes it was centuries old.

"If nothing else," he summed up, "the forest is a great place to hide. It'll be hard for the enemy to find you there, and you can build up an army under cover of the trees. When you emerge, it'll set the shamans into a panic. Chaos will spread among them, for surely they'll not be expecting use of the Mach Furr. They'll think you in Chatchek. Or if they learn from spies that you're on another quest, your secrecy means they'll not discover where, what or how."

That had been her plan. Without doubt, there were spies in her camp. They should not learn of this plan, but *should* not and *would* not were different things. It was possible one of the chiefs was working against her. She thought that unlikely, but it was possible. For that reason she had not told them exactly where she was going.

That night, after dinner, was the time set for their departure. Once more they convened in the secret room beneath the fortress. Only this time it was only the travelers who were there, and Kubodin to see them off.

Radatan and Huigar were armed profusely. Asana had only his usual sword. That, and the little statuette of Shulu that he always carried. Shulu had instructed him never to part with it, and he followed her orders without fail. Sometimes, as now, she could see the outline of it beneath his cloak. What its purpose was, she did not know. That it had one, she was certain.

Boldgrim was the last to arrive. Whatever he thought of this venture, he kept it to himself. But she could not forget his initial reaction, no matter that he hid his thoughts now. At any rate, he had agreed to it, which was all that mattered. Surely he would not have done so had failure been inevitable.

Kubodin hugged her. "Luck," he said, and that was all.

"Luck to you also," she answered. "Keep an eye on the enemy shamans. They *will* try something, I'm sure of it."

The little man and Asana then embraced, but they said nothing. Those two seldom did. Their friendship surpassed words.

"Are you all ready?" Boldgrim asked.

Shar looked around. They all seemed to be, and she noticed something that she had not before. Huigar wore a small flower in her hair. It would be a parting gift from her father. No doubt they had said their goodbyes in private.

Boldgrim gave them clear instructions. "Once the magic is invoked and the gateway opens, I cannot hold it that way long. You must pass through swiftly. I will go first, and then the rest of you, one at a time."

They got themselves ready, forming a line. Radatan would go straight after the shaman to act as a guard to him on the other side. Then Huigar as a guard to Shar. Then Shar herself. Asana would come last.

Boldgrim approached the far wall of the room. He stomped the end of his staff against the stone flagging toward each corner, and a violet light shimmered there. He did the same toward each corner of the ceiling, and likewise two spots of light glimmered in those places. Then he used the tip of his staff to draw a ring of magic, connecting the four points.

The shaman stepped back. Thrice he struck the floor with his staff, and some strange force crackled through the room as though a wind blew. Shar felt her skin tingle, and her hair stood on end. The ring of fire brightened with each reverberation of the staff against stone.

Bowing his head, Boldgrim muttered words of power. The ring of magic flashed and shimmered. Shar realized it spun like a wheel now. The spinning grew rapidly faster, and in moments it was too fast to see.

A strange noise filled the air, like the grinding of stones or the slow shifting of a mountain under its own weight, and then suddenly the spinning stopped.

A gateway shimmered before them. It was a tear in the reality of the world. Like an eye it was, peering at them.

Or peering from their world into another. For the wall behind that ring was gone. What showed there now was a shadowy and barren land.

"Swiftly now!" Boldgrim cried. And he leaped through the opening.

12. Voices in The Mist

The gateway winked like a giant eye as Boldgrim passed through. The forces of magic within the spell swirled and shimmered, reacting as an entity from one world entered another.

Moments later, it did the same thing in sequence for Radatan and Huigar. Then it was Shar's turn.

She did not remember drawing the Swords of Dawn and Dusk, but they were in her hands as she leaped forward. She felt the energy of the spell as the eye closed down on her, and like a pip from a fruit that was pressed, she shot forth into the void.

Mist swirled around her, and she could not sense any direction, nor even an up and down. Out of the mist, voices called. Some were beautiful and clear, while others were the fell cries of evil. Cold and clammy was the air, and she sensed creatures all around her, hidden. But they knew she was there.

Then she was through the mist and into clear, if dim, air. With a stagger and a stumble she found her footing on the other side. Radatan was just getting up. He must have fallen, and Huigar was on guard with her sword held aloft and circling to see if anyone, or anything, was near their point of entry into the void.

Asana came through behind her, and she made way for him, marveling as she did so at his balance and poise. His sword was drawn also, but he did not stumble at all. He merely shuffled forward in a fighting stance.

Boldgrim groaned. Even as Asana came through, the magic gave way and the great eye, shimmering with power one moment, blinked and was gone the next.

The shaman fell to his knees. Shar went to him. If he died, they were lost in this strange new world. No one else had the power to return them to the world of flesh.

His skin was cold as ice, and a vapor issued from his mouth as he breathed. It looked like he would pass out, but his held his staff with an iron grip, and it was planted firmly onto the rocky ground.

"Are you well?" Shar asked.

"It will pass," Boldgrim replied. "Look out for enemies. The magic will attract anything that is nearby."

Shar needed no further warning. She whipped around, gazing at everything nearby.

It was a strange land. It seemed like the darkening moments of twilight when the sun had sunk beneath the rim of the world but its dying light yet lingered. Or those breathless, drawn out seconds, when night was giving way to dawn but the sun had not yet climbed above the horizon.

There was no grass, yet the landscape was open. To one side, a series of rugged hills lifted up into a highland plateau. Everywhere else, the lands were mostly flat. In place of grass was a desolation of sand and loose rocks. Nor were there living trees, except here and there sickly stands of timber that thrust upward, skeletal-like and void of leaves, as though once they lived if even ten thousand years ago. It was like a plague of death ravished a once-fair land, and preserved it in its death throes for eternity.

There was nothing living to see. Yet still Shar kept a close watch. There were folds and gulleys in the land where many things could hide. And anything that lived here was born of the void, and who could say what its shape or nature would be?

Better to look instead for movement. That would be a surer guide. Everything was still though. Shar trusted it even less. She *sensed* they were not alone here.

"A dolorous place," Asana said quietly.

He was right. This was the void. Or at least one aspect of it. It was the realm of death, and a gateway between worlds. It was a shadow existence.

Shar looked upward. The sky was gray, but scudding across it were darker clouds. She did not think they would ever bring rain though. Not here. Or if they did, it would be poisonous. Perhaps that explained the dead-looking trees.

Boldgrim had recovered, and he joined her. His face was still drawn with fatigue though, and the skin around his eyes was pinched.

"Trust nothing in this land," he said. "Eat nothing and drink nothing. It is not safe here, and there are other perils than the obvious."

"That will be difficult," Huigar said. Shar noticed the flower in her hair had seemed to wilt since they had come through the gate.

"Why?" Boldgrim asked.

She pointed behind them to the rising cliffs. "Is that not the back of Chatchek Fortress?" She swept her arm out, encompassing the flat lands before them. "Are those not the Fields of Rah, where the Nagraks gather to besiege us in the real world?"

Boldgrim laughed, and the sound, like all their voices, sounded hollow in this desolate land.

"You are perceptive. Yes, the void is a shadow land. A reflection, of a kind, of the real world. We stand now upon the ground that serves as the foundation of Chatchek Fortress in our own world."

"Then we have a long, long way to walk to Nahlim Forest," Radatan said. "And we must eventually drink and eat what food we can find in this place."

"Not so," Boldgrim answered. "The magic that enables travel through Mach Furr is complex. You saw the mist when we came through the gateway? That is the true Mach Furr. That is the true gateway. We can enter that again in the void, and through that, to put it into a term you can understand, we can *jump* great distances here."

"All the way to Nahlim?"

"No, not that far."

"How long will it take?" Shar asked.

Boldgrim thought for a moment. "A day. Maybe two. It depends on what problems we encounter."

Shar knew something of this. "The Mach Furr, the mist, is more dangerous than even the void, is it not?"

"By far. The void is dangerous though. Deadly dangerous. But the Mach Furr is worse."

They each looked around with wary eyes. Still, nothing showed itself. It would be a fearful journey, and Shar was proud of each and every one of them. There was great danger here, but they had put that aside to help her. Or to help the Cheng Empire. Just at the moment, the two were one and the same.

"Well," Radatan said, "there's no point standing around. Let's 'jump' as you call it Boldgrim, and get going."

The shaman shook his head. "It doesn't work like that. The magic is not strong enough in all places. We must walk until we come across a suitable place where the magic remains strong. It is easier in our world, full of life. But in the shadow world of the void, all things are drained and at a low ebb."

"Except for evil," Shar added.

"Yes. Except for evil. The dark is its natural home, and it is stronger in the void than good. Shulu taught you well."

So she had, and Shar was grateful to her. She would have died many times so far without the skill and knowledge that her grandmother had imparted. Now, more than ever, Shar wished she was by her side.

It was time to move on, and they did so. They set forth in a westward direction, and trod the flat lands where, in another world that mirrored this, the Nagrak horde was gathered and laid siege to Chatchek Fortress. It bewildered Shar to actually recognize features of the landscape she knew, and yet at the same time notice that everything was different. There was no life here, nor any sign of the things, such as buildings, that life created.

The dust rose behind their passage, yet it settled swiftly. There was no breeze to disperse it. The air was stuffy, and did not seem wholesome. Yet travel was easy enough, and they made quick progress out onto the Fields of Rah.

It was there that they saw the first signs of life, if life it could be called. Horses roamed the plains, yet as the travelers drew closer to them the horses looked hostile. They pawed the ground and tossed their heads.

"Look!" Huigar called. "They're horses, but they're *not* horses."

Shar saw what her bodyguard meant. The horses were far taller than the ponies of the Nagraks, but they were slim. It seemed as though their sparse hide was wrapped tightly around their bones, and there seemed to be little in the way of flesh. Even, in places, she fancied she could see the white glimmer of bones.

Certainly their teeth stood out. They were not the teeth of horses, but rather the sharp-pointed fangs of predators. It made sense to Shar, for there was no grass here to graze. They must hunt flesh.

That thought put her on her guard, and she drew her swords. The others followed suit.

"See how they begin to circle us?" Asana said. "They're like wolves hunting a herd of deer."

"Do not fear," Boldgrim said. "I have power against their kind, and I think they sense it. They want to attack us, but they hold back too. There are other things in this land that are more dangerous."

Shar did not wish to meet those things, whatever they were. The horses were unsettling enough.

They progressed across the dusty plains. The horses wheeled around them, circling closer at times and at others moving farther off. Their movement raised great clouds of dust, making it hard to see, and it seemed like they did this deliberately.

"Do they seek to obscure themselves so they can get close and attack?" Shar asked.

"I have been thinking that," Boldgrim replied. "I can call upon a wind to drive the dust away, but I'm loathe to use power. The use of magic might be sensed by something that has greater strength than me."

They kept walking. Shar guessed, had there been a sun, that it would be mid-morning. Yet here in the void nothing had changed, and it was the same murky twilight that it had been when they arrived. The dust clouds were worse though, and it seemed that more herds of these skeleton-horses had gathered round them.

It occurred to Shar that herd was not the right term. Pack might be better, for she was certain now they were working together as predators.

Boldgrim thought so too. He raised his staff, and swung it in slow circles. A breeze picked up, fitful at first, and then it blew hard, driving dust before it and then funneling upward to disperse the dust high into the sky.

The horses trotted away, but another pack took their place on the opposite side. Again Boldgrim dispersed the dust, and they too retreated.

From then on, the horses kept their distance. Shar watched them closely, but she also looked beyond them and into the sky. She knew their passage through these deadlands could not go unmarked, and other eyes than the horses would soon watch them.

They came down into a gulley, and it was deep with dust. Yet in places round rocks showed, smoothed by some force, perhaps by wind and sand acting in conjunction, or maybe even rain. The latter was hard to imagine, yet there were clouds. If it rained here though, Shulu had never said so.

They came up the other side, and a pack of horses stood there. They were close now, only fifty feet or so away, and the bones of their ribs showed white in places through the taught hide that covered them. Shar did not think they were alive. Their eyes seemed like dark sockets, and when they neighed it was a grating sound like a whetstone against jagged steel.

The horses did not give way. Boldgrim yelled, and Radatan picked up a stone and cast it at them. This caused the pack to prance around in different directions, but then as one they darted forward and attacked. Their speed was as fast, or faster than an ordinary horse. The jaws opened, flashing white fangs. The thunder of their charge was as a roar.

Boldgrim raised his staff, preparing to work some magic. Radatan and Huigar closed in around Shar. Asana strode forward, sword deftly raised, but there was a light about him and then it seemed an aura formed from it and stepped out of him. It was a woman, cloaked and cowled. It was the same one Shar had seen before when it helped them on their journey to the Wahlum Hills, and she thought it came from the statuette. It could not be Shulu though, for the figure of light moved with speed and dexterity like a young woman.

Light flashed from the eyes of the strange figure, and nothing more. Yet that was enough to panic the horses, and they charged wide around the travelers instead, entering the gully and galloping out of sight.

The strange figure turned back to the travelers, but her hood was drawn close and nothing could be seen of her face. She bowed, seemingly to Shar, and then was gone in a shimmer of light.

"What magic do you possess, Asana Gan?" whispered Boldgrim with a certain reverence. "I have never seen its like before."

"I don't know. It's not mine, but a gift of Shulu Gan."

Boldgrim was going to ask more, but Shar decided it was better he did not know. She trusted him, with her life, but Shulu's secrets were her own.

"You can ask her, when you meet her. And I'm sure you will. This battle for the Cheng nation is in full flight now, and before the end I expect her to return. Until then, we'd better hasten on. I don't like to stay in the one place too long."

Boldgrim inclined his head by way of agreement, but from then on his considering gaze frequently happened upon Asana.

They had not gone far before there was a change. Shar could not quite tell what, but the air seemed different. It still had that dead feel to it, but now there was something else she could put no name to.

"We approach a place of increased magic," Boldgrim warned them all. "Stay very close to me, and if you hear strange voices … ignore them. No matter what they say."

Soon a wispy mist curled up from the dusty ground, and it was clammy around the legs of the travelers. Then a wall of fog became visible in the distance. There *were* voices in the air, and Shar fancied she even knew some of them. So far, she could not quite understand the words though.

The wall of mist began to churn and roil before them.

"This is a gateway through Mach Furr," Boldgrim said, turning to Shar. "If you still wish to risk Traveling, we must enter the mist."

13. Voices of Entrapment

There was no real choice now, and Shar knew it. Their decisions had been made back in the underground bowels of Chatchek Fortress.

"Speed counts," Shar replied. "Without it, we are lost."

Boldgrim straightened, and a look of determination chiseled his face.

"Then all of you, follow me. Stay as close as you can. And whatever you do, do not stray from the path I make. It will be dangerous, but to step into the mist is death. Not just of your body but of your soul. And you will be tempted to do just that. Resist, or you will die."

It was a stern warning. Shar did not doubt the danger. Shulu had told her that the lore said to die here was to destroy your soul as well. Even so, she wondered if that could be true. Nevertheless, the danger was extreme even without that.

Boldgrim lifted up his staff, and he stepped toward the wall of mist. It towered up above them all, imposing and terrible. The soft whisper of voices filled the air, but nothing could be made out.

Shar drew her swords. She would be ready for whatever came at her, but she did not think it would be a physical attack.

Boldgrim began to chant, and he entered the mist. The others followed after him, and Shar felt the cold embrace of the vapor like a searching touch of evil that played and toyed with a victim.

The bulk of the mist was kept at bay though. Boldgrim created a corridor as he walked ahead, and only here and there did dank tendrils twine into it.

Mist covered the ground, and the dusty surface could not be seen. Yet from the vapor glowed a faint violet light. That much at least was Boldgrim's magic, and it lit the way ahead, if dimly.

Boldgrim strode forward. He gave off an air of haste rather than fear, yet he, and the others, must feel what she felt. There were things in the mist.

Shar felt eyes upon her, and at times the fog roiled with hidden movement. Then shadowy forms appeared. Some seemed human, but many others were not. Some were small, and some vast creatures bigger than a bull. All pressed in against the corridor of light that cut through their shadowy realm, but Boldgrim's magic offered some sort of protective barrier.

The magic of the shaman did not block out voices though. She heard them more clearly now, and then a figure appeared in the mist more openly than the others. It was of a woman, tall and fair. Her hair streamed down like a raven's wings, and her eyes were lit with emotion. She wore a white dress, yet there was blood upon it as though a sword had pierced her flesh.

Asana, my beloved! Help me! I will die without you. Come to me, and hold me!

The swordmaster turned ashen, and his frame trembled. Shar had never seen him show much emotion, but now it was as though every feeling he had ever held in check raged through him in a wild torrent.

"It is not her," came the steady voice of Boldgrim. "Ignore it. It is nothing but a trick. Walk forward, and follow the path. Do not enter the mist!"

Asana hesitated, then he walked onward. He pulled his hood up to cover his face, and the beautiful figure pleaded with him a moment more, and then swiftly faded away.

Shar was shocked. It seemed to her that the apparition was of someone that Asana knew, and that there was a history there of high emotion. She had no time to think about it further though. A voice called to her through the fog.

Shar! I need you! Help me!

There was silence then, but a thick curtain of fog rolled away and revealed a terrible scene. Shar already knew the voice. It was Shulu, but nothing prepared her for what she saw.

Two figures were locked in combat. One was Shulu, and she was badly injured. Blood flowed from multiple wounds, and her breath came in haggard gasps. Her frail body was wracked with pain, and it was clear she was outmatched.

Shulu's opponent was a strange beast, terrible to behold. When it came into better view, Boldgrim hissed through his teeth, and Shar felt a nameless fear.

Madness danced in the creature's eyes, and it stalked the old woman on four legs before rising up on two to attack her. Shulu was knocked down, and the beast scrambled atop her, attempting to disembowel her with its raking back legs while at the same time to rip open her throat with massive jaws.

Shar! I need you! Have I not given you everything? Come to me before it's too late!

Shar felt an overriding desire to rush forward. This was not real. She knew that, yet what if it were? Shulu could travel the void. She had that power. It might be her in the flesh.

"Hold to the path," Boldgrim said, and there was reassurance in his voice. "It is a trick only. No matter what you feel, ignore it."

Shar gritted her teeth and walked on. The apparition was swallowed up by fog, but her guilt lingered.

So it went, and others of the travelers had a like experience, including Boldgrim. The magic did not protect him. Shar could not clearly see the apparition that appealed to the shaman, but it was a man of regal bearing, and she thought she guessed his identity. His voice, even threaded by agony as he clutched his stomach, was one of authority. Boldgrim pointed his staff and sent a blast of sorcery that scattered into the mist, dispelling the apparition and all others, for a time.

But the voices grew again, and this time there was not pleading in them, but anger. They did not show themselves though, and remained vague forms in the shifting airs.

"Behind us!" cried out Asana.

Shar tuned to look. There was a figure striding toward them, tall and heavy shouldered. It wore black robes, tattered at the edges, and a great cowl covered its head. Nothing could be seen of its face, and it made no attempt to talk to any of them. Rather, it hastened toward them down the same path they had just trod, and a sword, black and wicked, was held in its hand.

"Run!" came the cry of Boldgrim, and he raced ahead before them all. The rest followed, and the black figure lumbered ahead too, cumbersome in its gait but matching their pace, or even gaining.

In the mist, the figures shrieked, but Shar paid them no heed. She felt the menace of the thing behind her like a lash, and ran as fast as she could.

One moment they were in the fog, and the next they were out of it. It towered up behind them, and the voices wailed. For a moment they caught sight of the black figure, sword in hand and terrible to behold, then the mists thickened and hid him. They neither saw nor heard a thing after that.

They were in the open void again, dust beneath their feet and that strange twilight sky of scudding clouds above.

"Who *was* that figure?" Huigar asked.

Boldgrim rubbed his brow. "Put all you saw from your mind. They were phantoms only, and not real. Whatever is in your past, leave it there."

"That last figure was different though," Huigar persisted. "It was in the corridor with us, and your magic did not hold it at bay."

"No. I was not strong enough. Few would be. That figure ... I don't know who or what it was. It was some terrible warlock of the past I think, or something that once served the evil of the Shadowed Wars. It was *strong*. But that is in the past now. Come! Let us turn to the future."

Shar looked around. Her companions were pale and fearful, but Boldgrim was right.

"Where are we?" she asked.

They all looked around. It was the same as most places in the void. It was a shadow of the real thing, but there was nothing here that Shar recognized.

"I don't see a forest," she said.

"Maybe not," Asana answered. "But I think I've been here before. Everything looks different. Even so, I think we're on the lands that approach the forest. Perhaps a hundred miles away."

"So I think, also," Boldgrim said. "We have earned a rest and some food. Then we will walk again until I can find another place of magic where we can Travel once more."

Shar had no desire to enter the mists again. But they were not close enough to their destination yet to do anything else.

They sat on the dusty earth, and ate a meagre meal in silence. The rainless clouds flitted by above, and never did a breeze blow, an insect chirp or a bird call. It was an eerie place, and disheartening.

"How do you find your way in the mist?" Shar asked. The question was as much to break the dreary silence as for knowledge.

"It is the same magic that opens a corridor down which to walk. I must picture my destination, and hold it firm in my mind. Failure to do that … is dangerous."

They ended their meal, such as it was, and carried on. Once more the dust rose in a little cloud in their wake before settling down.

Ahead, there were some great ravines. Shar thought, perhaps, in the real world this was part of the Nightbringer Canyons. If so, they were on the far edge of the Fields of Rah and close to their destination as Asana had thought.

Boldgrim veered away from the canyons. No one needed to ask why. The void was dangerous enough as it was. Who knew what evil lurked in darker places such as that.

They saw nothing of the strange kind of horses that had attacked them earlier. But after a little while Radatan pointed above them, though he did not speak. It seemed there was something about the void that discouraged talking. No one wanted to break the deathly silence that weighed down over the twilight land.

Shar saw what he meant though. There was a flock of birds circling high above. They were not ibis but rather some kind of vulture. It was hard to gauge their size. They seemed small, but they were very high up. She felt that they might be huge birds, and they seemed to be following the travelers for their lazy spirals and occasional wing beats kept them ever directly above. And they seemed to be dropping in height, for they were growing larger.

Time passed, but it was hard to tell if it was a short or long period. Everything seemed the same in the void, and Shar had the feeling that if she slept here, centuries might pass.

The landscape did change though. Not the dust nor stifling air, but they now walked slightly downhill. Ahead of them, there was some haze, but it was too far away to see what it was. On their right the canyons opened up, black chasms like mouths that would swallow them if they went there. That they would not do.

Yet the denizens of those declivities came out to watch. At first there was one or two that stood on a ridge. Then ten or twenty. Now a hundred or so were there, and one figure seemed to lead them.

That figure was taller than the others, and massive. Ten feet high it stood, and it had hunched shoulders that spanned the width of a mighty tree trunk. In its hand was a club, and it looked on the travelers, gripping the club angrily and swinging it from time to time.

Boldgrim suddenly turned in the direction of the canyons.

"Are you mad?" Radatan asked.

"Not at all. I see what we need, and I head for it. Look, and you will see a patch of mist ahead. That is our escape. For surely I do not wish to fight anything from the canyons."

Shar saw it now. It was a small tendril of mist reaching up from a gulley. It was perhaps only twenty or thirty feet wide, but Boldgrim knew what he was doing. If he could use that to Travel, they would avoid a fight. For it seemed the massive figure on the ridge was urging something of the kind to the smaller creatures around it.

Boldgrim strode ahead. The creatures on the ridge, still growing in number, now shuffled down the slope to meet them.

The gulley was larger than it seemed, and so too the mist that boiled up from within it. Again, the travelers heard the calling of things within it, though no words were yet clear. They steeled themselves to enter.

The wall of fog blocked off their view of those creatures that came toward them from the ravine, but they could be heard too, calling to one another and urging themselves on.

"Best to get on with it," Shar said. "Else we'll have company, and I don't much feel like entertaining."

Huigar giggled, and even Boldgrim smiled. The tension was broken though, and the shaman lifted up his staff and led them into the mists.

Instantly, it was cold and clammy. There was an anger in the mist this time too that was not there before. It was like something within that sluggish gray vapor knew they had escaped before and held a grudge.

Boldgrim led them swiftly. He chanted as he walked, and the tunnel formed and glowed softly as before. They hastened after him, each haunted by the things they had seen last time.

And there were things in the fog again, whispering, but this time they kept a greater distance. For what reason, Shar was not sure. Perhaps it was because this journey was swifter, and they had not yet built up to it, for it seemed only a matter of minutes before Boldgrim strode out into the open again.

The fog was behind them, and the open twilight and dusty earth of the void was back. Shar had never thought to like it, yet it was better than the true Mach Furr.

It was not quite as open as before though. Dead trees, or trees that looked dead, leaned at strange angles and cast their dim shadows over the dusty ground.

"We are here," Asana said. "This must surely be the Nahlim Forest."

"Without doubt," Boldgrim said. "But now I must open a gateway for us to cross through to our own world. As you did in Chatchek, be swift to pass through. I can only hold it open briefly, and I am more tired now than I was then."

Shar glanced at him. He was pale, and the skin around his eyes was pinched tight. She even thought she could see some gray hairs in his beard that were not there before. Whatever strain he had been under to create the corridors through Mach Furr, it was greater than he had let on.

Nevertheless, he got to work swiftly. He followed the same procedure he had in the fortress, establishing four points of power and then bringing to life a circle of magic that spun, faster and faster, around them.

The gate opened. "Now!" he cried, and leaped through.

Quickly, the others followed. Once more Shar experienced that strange sensation of passing through. The gateway winked around her, propelling her to the other side. She felt the magic squeeze her, and it seemed she fell momentarily through mist, but then she tumbled to the ground and came to her feet, swords drawn.

Chaos was all around her. Boldgrim was trying to stagger up, his staff digging into the ground like a walking stick. The others had already sprung up, and had assumed fighting crouches. And Shar soon saw why. They were in a forest clearing, and just ahead of them was a line of warriors.

The faces of the warriors were shocked, as well they might be. Shar and her companions must have surprised them greatly, falling out of a bright light in the air that winked open, and now winked closed.

It was a situation fraught with danger, and not one Shar had expected.

14. A Glance Full of Evil

Shulu felt good. The shaman, puffed up idiot that he was, had appointed her to the position. Had he known that Shulu Gan was now a member of his household, his heart would have stopped with fright.

She smiled at him. He smiled back. Ignorance truly was bliss.

"Go and find old Nagrading. He's the one with snowy hair, and he'll be out in the practice yard somewhere. Tell him you now work for me, and he'll find you some livery, a room and give you your jobs from now on."

Shulu bowed, and walked from the room. Behind the shaman's back the witch-healer gave her the evil eye. It was a thing some witches did, and though it was a petty magic and below the notice of a shaman, there was a spell with it and some witches could cause great mischief.

The witch-healer was not one of them, yet it was still an attack and Shulu felt the urge to retaliate. Instead, she merely deflected the magic with an imperious gesture, returning it back upon the woman.

It was a time to be careful. The witch-healer was an enemy now, and she would be watching and waiting for a chance to take her revenge. It was nothing to Shulu, yet in the house of her enemies the last thing she wanted was scrutiny. If she could, she must try to make friends with the woman. Likely, that would be impossible though.

So be it. The woman had no real skill, but thought highly of herself. If she cast any more spells of bad luck, she would be taught the meaning of fear, no matter the consequences.

Out in the yard, Shulu looked around. There were several groups of men training, and each group was working hard. She admired that, even in her enemies. She could not see anyone with snowy hair, though.

She walked over the sandy ground, and sensed many eyes on her. She ignored them. They would discover who she was, or who she purported to be, soon enough.

Then she saw a glimpse of the man she wanted. He held a sword in his hand and he was showing a leg sweep to a group of young men. The shaman had called him old, which he was. Certainly his snowy hair showed that, for it was a rare trait among the Cheng except in advanced age, yet she noted he still had great dexterity.

She approached him. "You are Nagrading?"

He straightened smoothly, the sword poised easily in his hand. He looked relaxed and tranquil, but she did not doubt he was a great swordmaster. The best were always unassuming and calm, like Asana.

"I am, lady."

Shulu curtsied. "I am the new witch-healer. The shaman told me to seek you out, and that you will find me suitable clothes, a room and appoint my tasks."

Nagrading raised an eyebrow. "What happened to the previous witch-healer?"

Shulu shrugged. "Nothing, but now you have a better one. Make good use of me."

The old man did not show much in the way of surprise, and Shulu liked that too.

Nagrading casually threw his sword to one of the young men, who caught it deftly.

"Then come with me. The proper livery and a room will come first, then we'll put you to work. There's no shortage of injuries. And I fear we've had one death today, or will shortly."

"The man with the infected wound to his stomach?"

"Yes."

"Do not fear for him. He will live, and is recovering even as we speak. He'll be back in your training yard soon."

The old man raised both eyebrows at that, but then his momentary surprise was hidden.

Nagrading was of that silent warrior type. He said few words, but when he did speak his tone was courteous. He gave away little of what he thought, and even less of what he felt. Other servants greeted him formally, but with friendliness. They liked him, and so did Shulu. He reminded her of the warriors of old, and that even those who served the enemy might be good.

He was efficient too. In short order Shulu was dressed in the household livery of black with gold trimmings. She laughed silently at that, but could not have conceived of a better disguise if she tried. She did not look like Shulu Gan, Terror of the Shamans, just now. And that was well.

Nagrading also found an empty room for her. It was a simple and small affair, yet the waxed wooden floor was nice, the bed adequate and free of lice, and there was a window that looked out over the city. From here she could see much and get the fresh air she craved. It was not like being in the wild that she had always preferred, but it was better than being confined by four walls, which she had expected.

"There's a training session at sunset," Nagrading told her. "Come down for that and I'll introduce you to the men. Your skills will be needed, for rarely does a session go by without an injury."

"I'll be there, Master Nagrading."

The old man inclined his head, and closed the door to leave her time to rest. She did not need it, and sunset was some time away. He was being generous, and she liked him for it.

She opened the window and looked down. There was no one training now, at least in earnest. A few groups of warriors gathered around and spoke raucously, and here and there single men still practiced with a sword.

There was nothing to do for a little while, so she sat down on the bed and thought. Instantly, she felt tired. She was getting old, and all she wanted to do was lie down. Yet once she gave in to that type of weakness, it would become a habit.

Her mind stilled and her thoughts slowed. She reached out toward Shar, and then suddenly began to panic. She could not sense her.

It was not normal. Always she could sense her, if she tried. It was part of the magic that connected them. Yet if she were dead…

Shulu slowed her breathing and calmed herself. She would not give up on Shar. She would never give up on her. She *must* be alive. Yet if she had been killed, the shamans would learn regret. She would rain terror upon them such as they had never seen before.

That kind of thinking did not help her now though, and once more she calmed herself. Only then did she detect Shar's presence at the other end of her thoughts. It was faint though. Barely there at all. Was she ill or injured?

After a little while, Shulu realized what was happening. Shar had entered the void. For what purpose, Shulu did not know. Yet she had friends with her. That would offer some protection, but it was a perilous thing to do.

One of those with her was a shaman. Shulu did not trust him, yet Shar must. For that reason, Shulu was somewhat calmed. Shar was hard to fool, and she did not trust easily. The man had earned it.

Asana, as always, kept a close eye on her. That, Shulu could easily sense, and she was grateful. Bringing the swordmaster and Kubodin into this had been one of her finest decisions. Even so, the dangers of the void were many, and the shaman seemed young. She almost reached out to him with her thought, but decided against it. He would sense her presence, and she did not want that. There was something familiar about him though. More than most of the others of the Nahat.

15. The Silent Enemy

Kubodin brooded. Shar was gone, again. Asana was gone. And the enemy made ready for yet another attack.

Nor was it just any attack, but it was clear that they assembled now in massive numbers to try to take the wall. Almost, he thought, the shamans were so desperate that they might take the imprudent step of flinging their entire army at the fortress in one assault.

He almost wished they would. If they did that, and failed, their morale would be broken beyond repair. They would not attack again. And he might even venture out the gates to take advantage of their low point, and smash the army with force.

It would not happen, though. The shamans were too cunning for that. They were not great military commanders. Nor were the Nagrak leaders. Yet they had the skill to foresee where such impatience would lead them.

Even so, this would be a great attack. The defenders had seen off many before, but he could tell by looking at the men on the ramparts that they were nervous. They knew this would be a tremendous assault, and they feared it. They were right to fear it.

At the same time, a confidence had grown within them. They valued the rampart now, as they did not before. They had learned how to defend it. They had become practiced at defending it, and did so with skill and efficiency. The enemy was not likely to overcome them, and they would suffer great loss in the attempt to do so.

The enemy came on. Horns blew. Banners waved in the wind, and from somewhere at the rear a great drum beat out ominously.

They charged, and the noise of their approach became as thunder. It was a terrible sight to behold, for the oncoming warriors screamed battle cries and shook their weapons. They seemed fiercer and more determined than ever. The shamans had instilled blood lust in them, and they came forward in a fanatical wave.

"I wonder if the shamans have used magic on them?" Argash said. He was the only chief currently on the tower with Kubodin.

"It could be. Just maybe they did. This seems to be a near-final throw of the dice."

Argash nodded. He did not answer, for they both knew it meant two things, and there was no need to speak them.

The defenders might be overwhelmed this time. But if they were not, the shamans would become so desperate as to use magic. Against that, the defenders now had the Nahat, thanks to Shar. But they were only fifty, forty-nine since Boldgrim had left with Shar, and there were indications more shamans had joined the enemy. They could sometimes be seen at the rear of the besieging army, and at times, like just now, they could be seen speaking to the force about to attack. Their numbers were swelling, and it might be that they already had enough to overpower the Nahat, or at least try to. No doubt they had also taken pains to hide their true number so any such sorcerous attack might be more of a surprise.

Arrows thickened the air. Spears followed. Then came the time for rocks. All were sent winging, or dopped, over the ramparts. The result was death. The screams of the injured rose up to the heavens, and Kubodin ground his teeth. How many good men were dying? How many husbands, or sons, or fathers of children? And all so the shamans might keep their corrupt hold over a nation that should be free. It was ever thus. The rich and powerful played a game of chance with the lives of the brave and loyal.

The wave crashed against Chatchek Fortress in a fury of violence. It seemed the very stones of the citadel thrummed. Ladders were thrown up, and toppled with poles. Grappling hooks were cast over the balustrade, and the ropes they were attached to cut, or hacked when twined with wire.

Yet still they came. Driven to fury by past defeats, or urged on by shaman magic, or both, ladders, grappling hooks and attackers kept swelling in numbers until they gushed up over the rampart with red swords of wrath.

The defenders held their ground. They fought in silence and with calm born of past victories. They were hard pressed though, and fighting broke out across the top of the rampart as the enemy clambered over the wall.

"This might be the end," Argash said.

Kubodin admired his tone. He was calm, which was not easy. At any moment the defenders could be overwhelmed, and then a slaughter would begin. No one inside the fortress would be left alive save, perhaps, the chiefs who would be put on a show trial and then executed.

That was another certainty of war. The losers were criminals, and the victors wrote the histories, condemning the other side as traitors. The truth did not matter. Those who controlled the means of communication throughout a nation shaped its thought and taught its children. In a generation, a hero could become a villain, and a villain worshiped as a man of bravery and foresight.

"We *must* not lose," Kubodin answered, drawing his axe. "But if we do, better to be killed here and now in battle."

Argash drew his sword, and together they both watched. There was little else they could do.

The defenders on the wall had tasted of freedom though. Shar was their leader, and she united them but let them keep their tribal customs and chiefs at the same time. They had seen what the future could be, and they resented the yoke of the shamans who sowed discord in order to reap control. They had no desire to go back to that, and they fought for an emotion that was hard to define but they all felt it beat in their hearts and course through their limbs.

Kubodin sensed that feeling too. He caught the mood of the defenders, and he lifted high his axe and cried out in a mighty voice.

"Freedom!"

He shook his axe, and Argash joined him, holding high his sword.

"Freedom!" they cried together, and those on the tower with them took up the call, and the chant passed out over the battling men.

"Freedom! Freedom! Freedom!" The men on the rampart began to chant, and they slew as they called out the new battle cry that matched the mood of their hearts.

Yet still the enemy came on.

The stone of the battlement was slick with blood. The injured writhed. The dead lay still. The fighting danced back and forth over both alike, and no man asked for quarter nor gave any.

The Nagraks fought with courage and greater numbers. The defenders fought for a cause. Fate hung in the balance, and it seemed to Kubodin that even the gods must be roused to watch this, for the destiny of the land and of the people who dwelt in it was being decided.

One side won. The other lost, as always it must be. Kubodin felt a chill run through him, and his beating heart thrummed in his chest.

The Nagraks, once more, retreated. Like a spent wave they collapsed, all at once their energy diminished and they flowed backward, beaten and subdued, leaving a multitude of their dead behind them.

Again, the chant Kubodin had started grew loud, and the defenders cried out *freedom* over and over, but it was different this time. It had a tone not so much of a war cry now but a statement.

"The shamans will never win," Kubodin said. "Even if Shar is killed and this rebellion suppressed. Someone will spark it to life again, even if it takes another thousand years. The will of the people cannot be dominated once they know they have something worth fighting for, or worth dying for. All the shamans in the land are not enough to turn back the tide once it begins to flow."

Argash looked at him strangely. "I think you were touched by the gods, just then."

Kubodin knew better. "No. I was touched by the spirit of humanity."

There was much work to do after that. Many of the defenders had been injured, and they were rushed away to receive what care could be given to them. At the same time, more supplies were brought up to the rampart, mostly arrows, spears and rocks. Kubodin watched carefully, proud at how efficient the whole process had become.

He gazed out over the enemy. They were sullen and lifeless, as well they might be. The defenders must be prepared, but he did not think there would be another attack today. Maybe not for a long time. Nagrak pride had been injured, and the might of their army had been rebuffed. Worse, it had been crushed.

In their situation, Kubodin knew he, and any normal person, would be asking a simple question of the shamans.

"Why? For what purpose are we dying? Why do you cast away our lives as a farmer scatters grain in a plowed field?"

The shamans must now fear the army they gathered might turn upon *them*.

Kubodin walked the ramparts, speaking to the defenders and congratulating them on their victory. Always he sowed the idea of hope. Shar was on another quest, and she would bring more allies. This war would not last forever. One day, perhaps not that far away, they could go home. And they would do so as free men and part of a prosperous empire.

He was returning to the tower to make a closer watch of the enemy when a messenger came. It was a young man he did not recognize.

"Are you General Kubodin, sir?"

"I am lad."

The young man bowed. "I bring news from our regiments in the high ridges behind the fortress."

Kubodin knew at once it was not good news. The messenger showed signs that he had been in battle himself, though he was not wounded.

"Speak, then."

"The enemy have been harassing us, but you would have reports of that already?"

"Yes, for the last few days."

"What is new," the young man continued, "is that they have managed to get more troops into that high country, and our own are now sorely pressed."

It was not unexpected. Despite the ruggedness of those hills, cutting the fortress off from supplies was a crucial tactic. The enemy should have done so sooner. He knew Shar would have.

The question was whether or not it was worth fighting to keep their supply lines open longer. It was a relatively easy decision though. Because of Shar's prudence, they already had a great deal of supplies. Food, the most vital of all, was stored in enough abundance that the fortress might survive a year or longer, even completely cut off.

Even more would be better, and Kubodin did not relish the idea of being isolated. Even so, was it worth keeping men there to fight? At best, they would only last a few days more, and in the scheme of things the benefit in terms of supplies was as nothing.

"Are you well enough to return lad?"

"Yes sir."

"Then go back, and give word that I order a retreat back into the fortress."

The young man left, but Kubodin did not trust the chances of war. Accidents could happen, so he summoned several more messengers and gave them the same instructions.

It was a sobering thought though. Chatchek Fortress would soon be cut off from the world. Once again he saw Shar's foresight at work, for she was already moving to solve the problem before it had even started. If she were successful in beginning a rebellion elsewhere, the enemy's forces would be divided. Did they really have the numbers to deal with a new threat, and still keep Shar's army penned up here? He did not think so.

He made his way back to the tower. The defenders almost seemed cheerful, and well they might be. They had thrown back the Nagraks, defied the shamans and still lived. It was as close to a victory as you could get while stuck in a fortress.

From the tower he looked out over the Fields of Rah. It seemed the Nagrak's numbers had grown despite their many dead. Probably they had, for reinforcements must still be coming in, and maybe other tribes were summoned as well. It did not really matter, now. The defenders had been through the worst that warriors could throw at them. They would endure more. What worried him most was the shamans.

For the rest of that day there was a brooding quiet from the enemy camp. They were sullen and lethargic, yet messengers could be seen going to and fro between various parts of the army. What was being discussed, only they could know. But their numbers and their hurried travel bespoke of a violent disagreement.

Dusk fell, and the tranquility of the setting sun and reaching shadows cast a peaceful look over the landscape. It covered up the bloated bodies of the dead, hidden in the deeper shadows at the base of the wall, but it brought the stench of corruption more strongly to the defenders.

The night passed. Several times Kubodin was woken by his aides when reports came in from those defenders who guarded the high country behind the fortress. By dawn, they were back in Chatchek, and all ways in, or out, of the citadel were closed. They were sealed off from the world now, except for what the Nahat might do.

For their part, the Nahat remained inscrutable. Boldgrim had dared to enter Mach Furr, but the rest of the Fifty showed no inclination to do so. Certainly, they could never bring much in the way of food or supplies to Chatchek. News of what was happening in other lands might be far more important though, yet it seemed they were content to await Boldgrim's return. And if he never did, it was a warning to leave the perils of Mach Furr alone.

Something must happen today, one way or another. Kubodin sensed it in the air. It felt charged, as though a storm approached, and he, like everyone else, felt it.

Yet after a hurried breakfast and a walk up the tower stairs to the top of the battlement, he saw that the enemy encampment was still quiet and subdued.

He did not like it. It would not, could not, last.

There was no sign of a military advance. The warriors were seated and playing at dice or talking. The next attack would be one of sorcery, as he had feared. Nor any sorcery. He knew it in his bones. There were Nahat here to protect against that. No. This would be some dark magic. Forbidden. Terrible. Something even to break the Nahat.

16. Touch the Swords

Shar glanced around quickly. The forest clearing was lit by sun, and it seemed sometime around noon. The light was bright in her eyes after the void, and they began to water.

Of more concern was the line of warriors. They were Cheng tribesmen, but they seemed short and slight of build. Their clothes and weaponry were different too, favoring slender blades, spears for throwing rather than thrusting, and graceful bows. Many carried no weapon at all save a quarterstaff. Yet like all Cheng that Shar had met, no matter where, they looked as if they knew how to use their weapons with killing skill.

Taken by surprise as they must have been by figures appearing through a gateway of magic, they did not attack though. They seemed shocked, as well they might be, and at a loss for what to do.

Yet one of them, taller than the others and resplendent in a cape of fine fur and a deer-hide cap, reacted faster. His sword he threw down, and he bowed deeply.

"Forgive us, O gods. We were surprised by your sudden appearance."

Even as the man spoke he gestured for his men to sheath their weapons. This they did, and they bowed also, if not as elegantly as their leader.

Shar stepped forward. She lowered her two blades, but did not sheath them yet.

"Be at peace," she said. "I am not a god. Nor are my companions. I am Shar Fei, heir to Chen Fei, and I am the destiny of the Cheng nation."

The men looked at her, and they could not have been less surprised than they were when she emerged by magic into their camp.

Shar studied them some more. She knew them now. They were of the Roaring Stag Tribe, and they were one of many tribes in the vast forest and wide lands about. They were enemies of the Nagraks, and had long held the much larger tribe at bay. Some of that was shamans' work, for they wanted different and divided tribes rather than the obliteration of them. Some was the forest itself, for the Roaring Stags knew their own home, and slaughtered by slow ambush and woodsmanship any raiding armies that entered. Most was down to their skill, for it was said they could hide in the forest better than a mouse under a bush and were more fearsome than a roused bear in battle.

Their leader studied her in turn. She saw him take in the twin swords, and then how his eyes widened as he looked into her violet ones.

He came closer, peering at her and blinking as though to clear his vision.

"Her eyes!" he called out to his men. "Look at her eyes!"

He spoke in a dialect that was easy to understand, but he pronounced many words differently from what Shar was used to. All his men were studying her, and she sheathed her swords with a flourish and winked at them.

The man bowed again. "Is it possible? Aren't you fighting the Nagraks somewhere on the other side of the Fields of Rah?"

"Many things are possible when destiny lays down a path to walk. I have just come from fighting Nagraks, and shamans, and beating them both. But the grip of the shamans over the tribes extends far and wide. I have come here now, to the Nahlim Forest, to bring your people on the same path I walk. It will take you to freedom and prosperity."

The man looked at her, and she read admiration in his gaze. She saw a similar thing in most of his followers.

"How may we serve?" he said simply.

"Take me to your chief. Send no word ahead, for my coming will then be reported, one way or another, to your clan's shaman, and that I do not wish. I will confront him, face to face, when I get there and give him no chance to set a trap for me."

"It will be as you say," the man said. "Our head village is two days from here though. Would you like to eat, first?"

Shar read no deception in his features. There were a few of his men that she mistrusted though, and she knew she must count them all and keep an eye on them. Likely some would slip away and take word to the shaman. There were always some like that.

"We'd be pleased to have some lunch. Our journey here has been ... tiring. What shall I call you?"

"I'm Nomak," the man answered.

"Then, Nomak, I fancy I already smell something cooking."

They went to the center of the clearing where a fire was burning, but it was mostly burned down to embers. On the far side a pit had been dug, and it turned out a wild pig was cooking inside it, heated by stones and covered by broad green leaves to create steam, and sealed over again with more green leaves and earth.

Introductions were made all around, and when Asana gave his name there were many bows and gestures of greeting. Shar made sure to count all those present, and there were twenty-four. None had yet had a chance to slip away, but she was watching.

The Roaring Stag warriors were different from all others she had met so far in her travels, but Shar liked them. They were quick to laugh, and seemed of an open nature. Shulu had told her as much, but she had also warned they had long memories when it came to grudges.

They feasted when the wild pig was brought out of the earth oven, and drank of the harsh ale the Roaring Stag tribesmen favored. It turned out these warriors were a kind of scout, similar to the Leng Fah in Tsarin Fen. Shar felt an affinity for them, and she was keen to see how they traveled through the forest and what skills they displayed.

After eating, they rested. Shar felt a need for haste, but forbore saying anything. So far, there were still twenty-four of them, and no one had slipped away to warn the local shaman. As long as that was the case, there was no real hurry. Also, she did not want to give off a sense of urgency. It would go against her if the chief wanted to negotiate.

Midafternoon saw them scrape earth over the remains of the fire and slip into the woods. The soil was chalky, and the forest was an ancient beech wood. The tall and stately trees towered above them, their smooth trunks often covered by a pale moss that enhanced the sense of their age. This was an old forest, and the earth underneath their boots was thick with eons of fallen leaves and timber.

The season was turning though, and the trees were losing their leaves. The endless cycle was beginning once more. Everywhere Shar looked was the glimmer of bronze-gold leaves, and she loved it. Nahlim Forest was so similar to her home in the fen, and yet so different at the same time.

The Roaring Stag warriors, once they began to move after resting so long, did so with great speed. They hastened ahead, and yet they did so in near silence. Some of them fanned out ahead. Some came up the rear. Most stayed in the center near Shar and her companions, and she sensed their curious eyes on her frequently. She was as strange to them as they were to her.

The autumnal woods were a delight, and there was a magic in them that Shar had never felt elsewhere. Not the magic of the shamans, but the magic of the land. This forest lived when Chen Fei was a youth, and before the Shadowed Wars and into times when men dwelt in caves and hunted for sustenance rather than farmed. Even then, it had been ancient, reckoning time by the fall of countless leaves as numberless as the stars in the sky or the unceasing ebb and flow of tides that lifted the ocean higher onto land. It was as old as Alithoras itself, and it had not changed in all that time.

Nomak spoke to her occasionally, and questioned her subtly of events occurring across the land. The Roaring Stags seemed a primitive tribe by some standards, but by others they were sophisticated. Certainly Nomak had a sharp mind, and though she sensed his liking for her, and dislike for the shamans, he served his chief too. He was gathering what information he could about her so as to be able to answer the questions of his leader later, which were sure to come and would help inform the chief's decision as to which side to take.

Shar used the opportunity to let him know the details of the victories she had obtained in battle, and of who her allies were. She mentioned the Nahat, and the powers of the Swords of Dawn and Dusk. She gave off an air of certain victory, yet not of overconfidence. Victory would come only with hard work, sweat and blood. But to suffer the yoke of the shamans was to endure all three of those things as well. Only the ruling class was free of such hardship, the shamans profiting from others and keeping them fighting among each other so that their rule could continue.

She spoke of Shulu too, and hinted that she was working some great magic. It was not a lie. She knew her grandmother was out there somewhere, bringing to bear her powers to protect Shar and plot against the enemy. Perhaps it was with magic, or maybe some other means. Whatever the specifics, it was true in a general sense.

At whiles the warriors who carried bows loosed arrows at distant targets. Shar marveled at their accuracy. They said it was part of their normal practice, to train even as they traveled. Maybe that was so, or maybe they were trying to impress her. Either way, they succeeded.

Just on nightfall they came to a creek. It was not wide or deep, but to try to cross it would make for an uncomfortably damp night.

"No need to worry!" Nomak said, reading her expression.

He led them along the bank a little way as the long shadows crept through the forest, and there they found a kind of bridge. It was a tree that had been felled, and its once stately trunk now spanned both banks.

"Careful," Nomak warned. "It's slippery."

They went over in single file. Quite a few of the tribesmen carried only a quarterstaff for a weapon, and they held this horizontally as they crossed for balance. Shar understood why when it was her turn. The trunk was rounded, smooth-barked as beech trees were, and slippery from moisture and moss. Nor was it as wide as it seemed from the bank. Crossing by this means was difficult, but she was determined not to fall. The discomfort of that would be annoying, but more importantly it would be a bad look for one who claimed the right to be emperor.

She did not fall. Walking slowly but smoothly she crossed, and she joked with Nomak who waited on the far side for her.

There was a clearing close by, and there they built several fires. These were smaller than the single one at lunch, for they would not cook on them. They had kept meat from their earlier feast, and this was shared around as their dinner.

Shar felt deadly tired. She did not know what measure of time had passed while she and her companions were in the Mach Furr, for there was no day nor night there. Yet sleepiness kept creeping up on her, and she suspected it had been a very long time since she had rested properly.

They talked into the night, as campers around fires did, and Shar dozed off several times. Then she grew alert. When it was time to sleep, she kept a watch while her companions from Chatchek slept. It was not that she did not like the Roaring Stag warriors, or Nomak, but prudence required caution. She was in a strange land with only a handful of known allies.

She woke Asana when she could not fight sleep off any longer, and so they kept up a guard all night.

Dawn crept through the forest after an eventless night, making the moss-covered trunks seem to glow with a pale green light, while the bronze-gold leaves shimmered. After a swift breakfast, Nomak led them out again, and Shar was glad to see that the Roaring Stags were still twenty-four in number. She could have told Nomak her fears, but then she would have appeared weak in his eyes.

They moved through the forest swiftly. All day they traveled, and a few times there was a scent of smoke in the air. Shar saw nothing, but there would be villages close by. There were trails, some nearly roads. Most of the paths they followed though were narrow, only wide enough for one person at a time.

The land was largely flat, although at times there were small hills. From the tops of these, when there was a clearing, Shar marveled at the sea of gold all around her.

Toward dusk, the scent of smoke grew very strong. This would be a large village, no doubt where the chief lived, and their final destination. She prepared herself, and she requested Boldgrim when she had a moment alone with him to be ready to make a gateway. If things went badly, they would need a means of escape.

Shar was amazed that no one from Nomak's party had yet slipped away, but he now gave orders for a single messenger to go to the chief and explain who would shortly be his guest. Shar heard those instructions and she knew that Nomak understood her situation, and was trying to help her. He was very clear to the messenger that this news was for the chief's ears alone.

Of course, it was possible that he had given the messenger secret, and different, instructions earlier. She did not think so, though.

Night had fallen by the time they came into the village. It was different from what Shar expected. Many of the huts were built on tall poles, and they had wooden floors. In some places dwellings had been made between the branches of mighty trees, and these were accessed by rope ladders.

"We come now to the chief's hut," Nomak told Shar. "He's an old, old man, but his mind is strong and his wisdom great."

Nomak dismissed many of his men. Four only came with him, and their guests, as they ascended a rope ladder to the chief's hut. Nomak went first, and there was a muffled exchange of words with the guards at the top of the tower. Then the travelers entered.

The hut was larger than it seemed from without. There were several rooms, and they were lit with lanterns. There were windows too, with wooden shutters, but these were currently open. Through them Shar looked out on the sparkling lights of the village, for the most part below, but there were some other of these tree huts nearby too at a similar height. It seemed that she looked down upon a starlit sky, and it was very strange to her.

The chief held all her attention though. He sat in an intricately carved chair, polished and oiled. The timber was not beech, for it was very dark. It looked like walnut, but Shar had only rarely seen that timber.

His eyes were the same color, and they fixed on her with great curiosity. He was not awed as some of Nomak's men had been, and Shar instinctively liked him.

She did not bow, but inclined her head. Nor did she speak. She was Nakatath, and it was for others to address her first.

The old man smiled, and his eyes reflected his emotion.

"Welcome to the Nahlim Forest, Shar Fei. I cannot yet call you emperor, for you have not yet beaten the shamans."

He might not call her emperor, but he did not seem inclined to dispute who she was.

"That's fair enough, I think." She spoke to him informally, reading that his nature was like that, and that pomp and pride would only alienate him. "I have an army of many thousands, and not one of them calls me emperor either. When the crown is on my head will be the time for pretty words. Now is the time for hard deeds."

His smile widened, either because he appreciated her attitude or he understood how she was positioning herself in a place of authority, and not someone to be taken lightly despite her informal tone.

"Where is your army now?"

It was a fair question, and she appreciated that he grasped the situation perfectly. He *knew* her army was not anywhere near these lands, and if he were to join her it was because he chose to and not for fear.

"My army? Which one? I have one fighting the Nagraks even as we speak. The enemy throw themselves against the walls like a tide of blood. They will not prevail."

It did not hurt to remind him she was fighting Nagraks at the moment, for most of the tribes in the Nahlim Forest disliked them intensely.

"And what of the second army?"

"Why, that's my reason for coming here. This is where I will start gathering it."

The old man laughed. "I'll say this for you. You're bold!"

"Perhaps, but I'm merely telling the truth. I will raise an army in the forest, and the surrounds, and I'll squeeze the shamans between both forces."

What reply the chief was going to give, Shar did not learn. At that moment there was a commotion outside, and a man stepped through. Two guards were with him, and they were nazram. The man himself was a shaman, and he looked angry.

"What is the meaning of this, Maklar?"

The old man did not look so relaxed now. The smile was gone from his face, and fire flashed in his eyes.

"I could ask the same of you. Why do you come bursting into my home unannounced?"

The shaman looked around, and like a mask was drawn over his face he hid his arrogance and anger.

"I have heard urgent tidings, and I thought you would need my wise counsels. I have come to help?"

The old man looked at the shaman, and then at Shar. He had not quite made up his mind what to do yet.

"Let me introduce you two," he said. "Nachtar, this is Shar Fei. Shar Fei, this is Nachtar, shaman to the Roaring Stag Clan."

Shar gazed insolently at the shaman, a faint smile hovering on her lips. She would see if he could be perturbed into saying or doing something hasty. If it came to a fight, and she hoped it did, she would kill him, and his guards, swiftly.

Nachtar was not so easily manipulated though. He ignored her, and spoke softly to the chief.

"My wisdom is certainly needed here. As all know, Shar Fei is currently hiding in a fortress, on the other side of the Fields of Rah, too scared to come out and fight. She will soon be brought forth for execution, though. This, whoever it is, must be an imposter. Leave her to me, and I will soon get the truth from her."

Shar straightened. "There's no need for torture, shaman. Though I guess, given that you approve of the killing of women and children, torture might serve as a prelude for you. If you want to know the truth of who I am, touch my swords and die."

The nazram stepped forward and drew their swords. The shaman stepped back.

Shar made no move, nor did she take her eyes off the shaman.

"Dog," she said. "If your two littermates take one more step toward me they will die. Call them off."

The two nazram looked eager for a fight, but there was doubt in their eyes too. And surprise. They had never heard their shaman spoken to like that.

The shaman muttered a word, and the two men sheathed their blades.

"Good puppy." Shar said. Perhaps she was taking this too far, but she must show Maklar, and his tribe, that she had the power to thus address shamans, and that she did not fear them. Something of her attitude would catch with them after that.

"I don't propose a fight," she continued, "though if you attack me there'll be one such as you've never seen. I merely propose a simple test. You know the magic in the Swords of Dawn and Dusk. You know only I can wield them, and their touch is death to any other who tries to grasp them. If you doubt who I am, Nachtar, shaman of the Roaring Stag Tribe, come and place your hand, even for a second, upon one of the blades. Come now! Show yourself as either a liar, for you know who I am even if you don't know how I'm here, or a base coward."

17. Rise, and Be Ready

The shaman looked indecisive. The situation was quickly spiraling out of control. He arrived at a decision though, and tried to regain his authority.

"Take hold of her," he instructed the nazram. "I will question her in the jail house, and get to the bottom of her lies."

Shar drew her swords with a flourish, and her companions stepped closer to her. The nazram hesitated. They were outnumbered, and Shar's earlier threat must have been on their minds. They would have heard stories about her.

"Do it!" yelled the shaman.

"Hold!" countered Shar. "Is this how guests are treated in the Nahlim Forest? Shulu has told me often of this tribe's hospitality. Was she deceived?"

At last, the chief spoke. "It seems, Nachtar, that your nazram have greater sense than you do. They have no desire to die, and die they would. We all know this is the real Shar Fei. Who else would speak to shamans, and *chiefs*," he emphasized that last word with a wry smile, "in the manner she has?"

"Maybe she is, and maybe she isn't. Either way, she's shamans' business and I will have my way."

The chief stood. There was anger in his voice now. "Be silent! Shaman you might be, but your role is to advise and not decide. I am the chief of this tribe, and I will not have my guests treated so. If you have the courage, place your hand on her sword. It's a simple enough test. If nothing happens, you may take her away as you wish. Either that, or begone. You were not invited here, and your presence begins to offend me."

Nachtar grew red in the face, and his hands clenched in anger.

Shar smiled sweetly at him, but there was the promise of death in her eyes. He was not alive when Chen Fei, and all his kindred, were assassinated. She knew the description of all those – they were emblazoned in her memory by Shulu. He shared in their guilt though, to some degree, for he had not repudiated them.

The shaman had no choice. He did not wish to die, and he knew he would if he touched the swords. Nor did he have the strength, with or without the two nazram, to attack her. He knew that too.

"Forgive me, O chief," he said. "I have given my advice, and your wisdom has proved the greater. I shall withdraw."

He offered a perfunctory bow as he left. He did not look at Shar, but she sensed his seething anger. Nothing had changed here. His intention had been, and remained, to kill her. All that had changed was his tactics to try to do so. He would move now to something else.

The nazram ignored her too. But they looked relieved. Shar almost felt sorry for them. Anything they did would be done at the behest of the shaman. That was their duty, even if it got them killed.

When the shaman was gone Shar turned to the chief. He was sitting again, and his good humor seemed to have returned, for that faint smile played over his face again.

"If I had doubted who you were before," he said, "Nachtar has removed all doubt and confirmed you as Shar Fei himself. The more he wanted to kill you, the more I believed who you were."

"They all want to kill me," Shar replied. "They've tried many times, and failed. I'm a hard woman to kill. Worse luck for them."

The chief invited them all to sit, and chairs were brought. Introductions were made, and Maklar greeted them all courteously, especially Asana. Boldgrim was greeted kindly too, but at Shar telling the chief exactly who he was, the old man raised an eyebrow in surprise.

"I really am who I say I am, Chief Maklar," Shar said to him. "War ravages the land, and I want to end it as soon as possible. This is our chance at freedom from the shamans. Perhaps our only chance. Will you help me?"

It was a simple speech. Shar could be eloquent when she wanted to be, but she also knew how to judge her audience. Maklar was a kindly old man, wise in the way of the world and appreciative of straight talking.

"Tell me how you got here," he countered. He was still making up his mind, and this was to delay answering her question.

"You know Boldgrim is a shaman, though not of the group that currently rule throughout Cheng lands. He has powers that the shamans you know don't. He took us, in the flesh, into the void. There we traveled through the mists to come here."

The chief thought on that, and frowned. "I don't pretend to understand the magic, but I can see great advantages in it. No doubt it's dangerous though."

"Very," Shar said.

The old man nodded. "You like to live dangerously, don't you?"

Shar considered that. "For myself, I would rather be safe. I'd love nothing more than to stroll through your forest and explore it, making no harder decision than where to set up my camp of an evening. But for the Cheng

Empire that was, and that could be again, I will risk anything."

It seemed to be a good answer, for the chief sat back in his chair and nodded.

"So, you have an army? And your own shamans?"

"Both," she answered.

The old man looked at her in silence for some time. At length, he stood.

"What I do now," he said, "I do not do because of your army and your shamans. I trust little in such things. Armies can be beaten and shamans can change sides. Instead, I trust to destiny. It is written on your face and flows through your words. *You* are the rebellion. *You* are the spark that sets it alight. *Yours* is the guiding mind that drives it forward. In *you* I place my trust, and the wellbeing of my people."

The old man went on one knee then. "I will serve you, Nakatath. The Roaring Stag Tribe belongs now to the empire that shall be."

Shar felt a heavy weight settle over her. This was what she wanted, but the old man had brought it home to her with clarity. *Armies can be beaten and shamans can change sides.* The gulf between what she strove to attain and how things might turn out was still vast. And if she failed, men like this chief and tribes like the Roaring Stags would plummet into the abyss, and it would be her fault.

"I will not fail you," she said, and a rush of determination flowed through her. "Whatever it takes, I will do it."

They swore their oaths then, for loyalty and service went both ways. Her duty to him and his tribe was as great as theirs to her. If not more, for in the end an emperor was but a servant who served the greatest number of people, and that was the only reason why they were great.

"Rise, and be ready," Shar said. "Now we will see in truth who commands your tribe, for while we have talked the shaman will have gathered his nazram and conceived a plan. He will kill me if he can, and now you also."

18. We Must Be Swift!

The old chief sent messengers out, and they raced through the night. He had requested those loyal to him to come to his hut, armed and ready to fight.

Shar mistrusted the shaman though. His breed was slipperier than a fen eel.

"I don't think," she said to the chief, "that Nachtar will summon all his nazram and loyalists from afar."

"How else can he overthrow me then, if not by swords?"

"He might use sorcery."

"Impossible," the chief answered.

"Not so," Shar said. "They have used it against me and my army. They are willing to break all rules to secure their power."

The old man seemed shocked. "For shamans to use magic against warriors is unheard of. Truly, they've done this?"

Asana spoke. "My lord, they've done it. I've seen it myself. When it comes to Shar, they'll risk anything to kill her. Even fanning the flames of rebellion. Without her, there is no rebellion."

That gave Shar a thought, and she did not like it. "He may try other ways first. For instance, he might set fire to the tree in which this hut is built. We're vulnerable until more of your men arrive. We should get down from here at once."

The old man hesitated only a moment. Then he gave a quick sign to his bodyguards, and they leaped into action, exiting the house and going down to secure the base of the tree.

It was not long before the sound of fighting came up to them.

"Quickly!" Shar said. "If they win or lose, it's still better for us down there."

The others went first, climbing down the ladder, and Shar came last, assisting the old man.

When she reached the bottom section, a light sprang up and Shar saw that her caution was warranted. The light came from a lantern that one of the chief's guards had lit. He was wounded, for blood soaked his tunic, but he seemed to move freely. The injury must be superficial only.

By the light of the lantern she saw the other guards surround the base of the ladder, those of them that yet lived. The others were dead, laying still on the ground. Nor were they the only ones. A group of other men were there too, nazram most likely. Near them was a heap of twigs and branches, piled around the trunk of the tree.

"Hurry!" one of the guards called, seeing their approach. "There will be more."

Asana nimbly dropped to the ground, drawing his sword as he landed. The others followed, and the chief came down last. He looked around, and sadness was in his eyes.

"They were good men," he said. "Men who had guarded me for years. They deserved better than this."

"What now?" asked one of the guards who yet lived. He too was wounded, a gash dripping blood across his forehead. "Shall we go somewhere safer?"

"No," the chief replied. "Soon this will be the safest place for us. The men I have sent for will come here first. They'll not be long. If we go elsewhere, the shaman's men might find us first."

It was sound reasoning. But their allies were not here yet, and if the shaman gathered more men to attack, the chief would be hard pressed.

Shar drew her blades, and they glimmered in the lantern light. It was a tense few moments, and they backed up toward the tree trunk to put some protection behind their backs.

There was noise within the village, but it was hard to see anything. There was shouting, and it drifted up in different places throughout the forest, but it was hard to tell how close it was.

Soon came a gathering of warriors though, perhaps twenty strong. They carried torches, and they hurried toward the hut.

"Are they friends or foes?" Shar asked one of the chief's bodyguards who was close to her.

"I cannot tell," he replied.

The warriors came closer, and now the light of the torches revealed them better.

"Enemies," the bodyguard said.

As they drew closer, Shar could tell by the way they dressed that they were nazram, and it seemed to her that there was a figure behind them. Perhaps it was the shaman. He would hang back and let others die for him, but if she got too distracted he might attack her directly with sorcery. She must guard against both steel and magic.

The warriors drew close, and then they charged. Asana met them first, his slim blade sweeping out and killing two men before they even realized what was happening. He was a dim figure, a shadowy form that moved with inhuman speed, seeming like a god of war and death.

The charge of the enemy was slowed, as much by shock as by the death of some of their number. Asana wheeled to the side, coming at them from a different angle, and Shar leaped forward, twin swords flashing, to attack in his place.

Huigar and Radatan were close to her. Some of the chief's guards were nearby also. The rest kept close to the tree trunk, closely protecting Maklar as was their duty.

It was a bitter fight. Shar slew a man that she did not know, and that knew nothing more of her than that the shaman commanded her death. He was not the only one.

The clash of blades filled the village, and the nazram were skilled. Yet Asana and Shar were far better, and they were greatly supported by their friends. Even Boldgrim fought, disdaining magic and using his staff.

The attackers began to fall back, their rush repulsed. One of them lunged at Shar, thrusting with what she took for a spear. It turned out to be only a staff such as many of the Roaring Stag warriors used. Even so, she jumped back nimbly out of the way.

He stepped forward from the pack of his fellows, bent on pursuing her. The staff came at her again, this time as a sidewise swing intended to crack her skull. Shar folded back the Sword of Dusk against the inside of her arm, and used this to block the strike. The force of it shifted her footing and she stumbled a little. Even so, she thrust the Sword of Dawn forward in a driving lunge.

The blade took her opponent below the ribs, and it slid up and toward his heart. She pulled the blade back, kicking out at him at the same time to help free her weapon, and he fell to the ground, dead, before he even touched the blood-slicked earth.

The fight was nearly over. It had not lasted long, but suddenly there were more cries and torches with their smoky, flickering light. By that harsh illumination Shar saw more nazram joining the fray, perhaps a number double the size of the first group.

It would be too many. Only Boldgrim could save them now by summoning a gateway to take them elsewhere. Yet in fleeing they might be stabbed in the back. And what of the chief? She could not leave him to die. Nor would there be time to explain the gateway was a means of escape.

Asana drew closer again, and together they leaped toward the new attackers, hoping to dismay them by a ferocious attack. It was a deadly play of swords, and blood misted the air. No one was as good as the swordmaster, but Shar was approaching his skill. Yet they, and Huigar and Radatan who joined them, were not enough.

Blood seeped into Shar's eye, and she wiped it away. She did not even remember taking a blow to the head, but she must have. Radatan limped, and Huigar was slightly crouched over as though nursing an injury to her body. For a few moments the enemy had almost broken and run, despite their massive advantage in numbers, but now they pressed in, and the defenders slowly retreated toward the tree trunk and the chief.

Shar could hear and see the shaman behind the press of warriors, exhorting them on. If she could only get to him, she would kill him. There was no way to do that though.

Again she stepped back, and again. She hated it, for retreat was not in her nature. But the enemy had not won yet, and even as she thought that there was more noise, and a large group of warriors joined the battle. They smashed into the enemy from the left side.

The enemy held though, but their momentum was stilled. Shar retreated no more, and instead redoubled her efforts. She drove forward, her swords gleaming wickedly in the night, and killed. She felt the lust of the blades, and the demons in them spilling the blood they thirsted for and getting the chaos and battle madness they desired. They would drink deep this night.

Nachtar called out, haranguing his men. He screamed at them, for he sensed that if he did not kill Shar and the chief now that soon other help might arrive and it would be too late.

The fighting was fierce, and the enemy warriors good. Yet they had learned to fear Shar, and none of them wanted to go against her. Of Asana, they had acquired a supernatural awe. It was only when the shaman forced them on that they attacked.

Shar tripped and fell over the body of a warrior, and one of the enemy thrust at her with the end of a staff. She dodged it, and came to her feet ready to fight, but the man eased back into the ranks of his brothers, unwilling to risk his life. He had seen her swift blades bring sudden death.

The shaman screamed and harangued. He came forward a little himself, and Shar could see him clearly now. She could not reach him though.

Even as she looked there was a warning cry from a warrior, and something flickered through the fitful light. It was an arrow, and it pierced the shaman's neck and came out the other side.

Nachtar clamped his hands to the injury, but blood spurted all around them. He made to speak, but when he opened his mouth a torrent of blood gushed forth. He fell to his knees, and then collapsed. All around him the nazram looked shocked. They had seen much death, but never had they seen, or even heard tell, of a shaman being killed.

The enemy were shocked, yet it seemed that one among their number began giving orders and organizing them to keep fighting, but a voice crackled through the night.

Shar stepped back, and risked a glance behind her. There she saw the chief. He held in his hand a bow, and it must have been him that had killed the shaman. Where he got it, she did not know. He might have taken it from one of his warriors, fearing they might not loose an arrow at a shaman, or wanting to himself after the shaman had tried to burn him alive.

Maklar handed the bow to a guard beside him, and his voice boomed out.

"This is shaman's work! Stop! There's no need for tribesman to fight tribesman. Stop!"

The fighting slowed and then ceased. The two forces separated from each other. Maklar spoke again.

"Nazram! Put down your weapons. I am chief here, and I command. I will forgive you for following the shaman's orders, but only up until this point. Do you hear me?"

They heard him, and they whispered among themselves for a moment. Then, grudgingly, they laid down their weapons.

More warriors were arriving now, and they were the chief's men.

"Tend to the wounded," Maklar commanded. "Remove the dead, and treat them with respect, nazram and warriors alike."

Shar was pleased. They were wise orders, and would help to ensure no further fighting broke out. She whispered in the chief's ear though, and he nodded in agreement to her suggestion, even if reluctantly. In turn, he gave orders to two of his guards.

The body of the shaman was brought to the trunk of the tree, and there tied. It was a gruesome thing to do, yet necessary. He had failed the Cheng people in life, but in death he would serve a purpose. Tomorrow the whole village would see him. Word would spread to other villages all through the forest. Shamans could be defied and killed.

"You're a hard woman, Shar Fei," the chief said quietly.

"Were I not, I would be dead. And do you think the shamans would slay me swiftly as you slew Nachtar?"

To that, the chief gave no answer.

It was dawn ere the bodies were cleared away and Shar was able to rest, sure in the knowledge that the malice of the shaman had been stopped. For word came in through the night of fights in different villages nearby, and there were those who decried the killing of the shaman, saying the blood of members of that order was sacred, and shamans were infallible rulers whose orders could not be questioned.

These were in the minority though, and fighting was quickly brought under control. Shar slept in the chief's house, and there was a heavy guard at the base of the tree.

She did not sleep long though, nor did the lively old man who headed the Roaring Stags. He called a meeting after breakfast.

"What now?" he asked. "The Roaring Stags are a free people again, ruled only by a chief, and I don't know how it works in tribes farther to the east, but here a chief who rules poorly can be set aside. That is freedom, but it won't last without fighting to keep it so."

Shar agreed. Freedom was not the natural state of humanity. Often those in power strove for more. If it were given them, then it was but a first step of many.

"Now," she replied, "I start a fire of ideas all over the land. I hold the east. We must build an army here in the west, and you are the start of that. Then between those forces we will crush the shamans. But we must be swift. Word of my presence here will soon reach the shamans, if Nachtar did not already warn them. They'll perceive my plan and move all powers under heaven to destroy us. They'll understand the deadly peril they now face, for where they outnumbered us vastly before, now I am in a position to even those numbers out."

Others were called to the council, and it became a council of war. Shar wished it would not be so, but the shamans would spill every drop of blood in the land before they ceded their power.

19. The Gathering of the Tribes

Sunlight came through the east-facing windows of the strange tree house of the chief of the Roaring Stags, and the angle of light kept changing as the morning passed. Yet still, they talked.

It was agreed that Maklar would gather as many men as he could from his section of the forest, and form an army.

Shar urged more. "Will you gather a delegation and come with me to a neighboring tribe? The Roaring Stags are only the start. We need others with us."

"Of course," the chief agreed. He would be feeling the pressure as much as Shar. If they did not bolster their numbers quickly, the enemy would destroy them. Like most tribes though, decisions were often slow in coming.

"What tribe will be most receptive to me?"

The old man scratched his head. "It's hard to say. These things are rarely discussed openly, but I think the Leaping Deer Tribe has little love for their shaman, and shamans in general."

"Where are they?"

"To our west, perhaps two day's march. Unless you want to take us there by this means of magic you have?"

Shar shuddered at that. "We'll walk. The magic has great value, but it comes with great risk too. It must never be relied upon, and only used in extreme need."

"Yet you used it to come here?"

"You can take that as a sign of how much I value the tribes of the Nahlim Forest, and what their joining to the rebellion means. I've had luck to get where I am. I openly admit that. The shamans underestimated me, but that's changing. They realize now what a threat I am, and I don't doubt that word would have soon come to your dead shaman to organize an army – and to march toward Chatchek."

"Well, an army will march, but not the one they intend."

There was a great deal of work to be done, and most of it fell to the chief. Despite his advanced age, his mind was sharp and his grip of the necessary information was strong. Armies did not march by themselves. They required provisions. Knowing what food stores there were, how much each man could carry, what wagons might take and how far the army could march with that, and where resupplies would come from, was tedious but vital work. The old man did it well, and Shar, listening in on many of the conversations found no need to interfere.

They left in the late afternoon for the Leaping Deer Tribe. Ponies were scarce in the forest, but one was available for the chief. The rest of the delegation walked, and Shar did not mind. She loved this forest, and she would enjoy walking through it.

The delegation was not large. Apart from Shar's group, and the chief, there were a dozen warriors as his guards. It was not that many, and evidently the two tribes were on a relatively good footing. Far better than most of the forest tribes were with the Nagraks.

While they were gone, the army would assemble and the supplies be brought in from various stockpiles throughout the clan territory.

Evening drew on, and it was cool. Shar pulled her hood up and wrapped her cloak tightly about her. Winter was getting close, and it would be hard to rouse the tribes in the cold weather to come. It was not fighting weather, at least traditionally. But like her forefather before her, Shar was not going to let weather, mountains, rivers, fortresses or enemies hinder her plan. She had a goal, and the sooner it was reached the sooner the tribes could go back to normal. If they survived. And the faster they acted the more likely that was.

They passed the night on a slight rise, ringed by the magnificent beech trees that formed the bulk of Nahlim Forest, at least in this section. Maklar set a good guard, and scouts were sent out to keep an eye on surrounding lands. The shaman was dead, and those forces loyal to him had surrendered, but it was always possible that others remained in the forest, unidentified and hatching mischief. The chief's party was probably too large to be attacked, but making assumptions was a good way to get killed. Shar did not, and she was pleased to see that the chief was cautious too.

The journey began again at dawn, and Shar looked skyward to see if there was any sign of their being watched by birds that the shamans might use. She could rarely see the sky though, for the tree canopy was still thick. It gave her some confidence that their movements were hidden, but she still worried.

The shaman had seen her, and despite what he had said he would have known she was who she claimed to be. Between then and when he was killed, there had been time to send word to other shamans. Perhaps by the nazram, or letter. If she were unlucky, he would have communicated by magic, and that would mean the enemy had learned of her presence here weeks before they otherwise would have.

She should have killed Nachtar the moment he entered the chief's hut. It would have saved her this worry, yet it was not her way. Nor could she predict how the chief and his tribe would have reacted to that.

The route they took began to slope a little downhill, and Shar thought there might be a creek ahead somewhere. She overheard some of the chief's guards talking though, and learned that they were approaching an area with several lakes, and it was near these that the Leaping Deer Clan mostly dwelt.

Radatan, near the front of the group, gave a gesture with his hand. Shar, and the rest, looked. Down below them in a fern-shrouded gully, shaded by tall trees whose leaves were spinning down in a golden rain, was a small herd of deer. They had not detected the humans in their forest world yet, but even as Shar watched the breeze stilled, then picked up again at a different angle. The deer lifted up their heads, caught the scent of predators and dashed away with grace.

Shar envied them. They recked nothing of wars and betrayal, of shamans and magic. But the winter would be hard for them, as was the one coming for the Cheng.

They moved ahead, and at whiles Shar walked beside the chief's pony. She did not let that time go to waste, and discussed with him the various tribes who lived in the Nahlim Forest, and their habits and peculiarities. Shulu had told her much, but the chief's information was more personal and certainly more current. If she were to rally these tribes together into a single army, as she had done before, she must make the effort to understand them and their needs. She could not lead by being who she was alone. She must also become what they needed.

They saw more deer at times, though never so closely again. The forest opened up a little, and here and there were open glades of grass. They crossed several small streams too, and these fed lakes which from time to time the travelers walked around.

Late in the afternoon, the Roaring Stag warriors grew more attentive. They were leaving their lands and approaching another tribe. The scouts out ahead frequently began to call out, mimicking the sound of a stag roaring during the rutting season, which was close at hand. This, Shar deduced, was to ensure the Leaping Deer warriors knew they were there, and were coming openly in peace and not mounting a raid.

They circled around a small lake on their left, and then crossed a bridge that spanned a small creek. The bridge was little more than a felled tree, but narrow ropes had been tied around it to ensure better traction for booted feet.

On the other side, some of the scouts were gathered, and ahead of them, in a large clearing, a group of warriors stood. They were not Roaring Stags, and this was immediately clear.

The warriors carried bows and spears, and wore the deer-hide hats that Shar was becoming accustomed to, but they also painted their faces with ochre to look fierce or otherworldly. Most of the ochre was green, but some was orange.

They came forward, and a young man was with them, taller than the rest.

Maklar whispered in Shar's ear. "The youth is their chief, Nogrod. He's only recently become chief, but I've met him once before. He has an old head on his shoulders despite his inexperience."

The new group came forward slowly. "Welcome to Leaping Deer lands," the young chief called out.

"Thank you for receiving us," Maklar responded. "We have great news."

Nogrod was close now, and his gaze took in Shar and assessed her. His was the only face unpainted, and that was well. He was handsome, yet no doubt there was a ritualistic reason the chief was unmarked, and nothing to do with showing his features.

"Word has come to me by the ways of the forest," the young chief answered. "I had not heard until now that you were good with a bow."

"Ah, I was in my youth. And it seems my skill has not deserted me over the years."

"It has not. Nor your daring."

Nogrod turned his attention to Shar and there was an emotion in his eyes that she could not decipher.

"You would be Shar Fei, then?"

"Indeed." She did not draw her swords to demonstrate it. She merely gazed deep into his eyes and let her violet irises prove what a thousand words could not.

Nogrod shivered. "Three days ago, ere any word came to us from Roaring Stag lands, our seer foretold that I should *gaze upon that which was forbidden*, to use her exact words. When our shaman questioned her, she would say no more."

"Your seer has talent. It has been death for a thousand years to be born with violet eyes. Even for those who are not of the line of Chen Fei. Such is the fear of the shamans. And yet for all their murder, you look now upon me."

He shivered again, and then went upon bended knee. His retinue did likewise.

"The Leaping Deer Clan is at your service, Nakatath. As am I. Long we have looked for your coming, and the stories of our ancestors whispered to us that the new emperor would walk among our tribe one day. We have, even if in secret, cherished those tales. And today, the legend has become reality."

Shar was surprised. She did not doubt that he was genuine, but the ease with which he had been won over was remarkable. Yet it was not her that had done it. This man, and perhaps his tribe, was in love with the *idea* of a new emperor. That enthusiasm might fade under the hardships to come. But she would take the easy victory, for without doubt there would be hard-fought setbacks in the future.

The two groups joined, and though there was some wariness between the warriors initially, it soon faded as they traveled.

Maklar and Nogrod set the example for they talked freely and with great friendliness, and that was no accident. They did it deliberately in order to set their men at ease.

Night was approaching, and they traveled to a spot by the sandy shore of a lake where fires had already been built and food was being prepared. There they sat and talked while the dark descended and the fires brightened.

"What of your shaman?" Shar asked the Leaping Deer chief.

"What about him?"

"Where is he? Will he try to cause problems?"

Nogrod grinned, and he suddenly looked even more handsome, but also somewhat more fierce in the deep glow of the firelight.

"He is gone, and none know whither. Doubtless he heard of the fate of Nachtar, and thought that was coming to him. Which it was." Nogrod grinned more broadly at that, and as much as Shar liked him, she would find him disconcerting as an enemy. Young as he was, there was a grim determination about him.

"Which tribe should I go to next?" Shar asked. "Who else will be as loyal to me as the Roaring Stag and Leaping Deer tribes?"

The two men thought on that as the smoke of the fire curled around them and a fish jumped noisily in the waters nearby.

"Perhaps the Silent Owl Clan," Maklar suggested.

"Maybe," Nogrod agreed. "It's hard to judge. The people all through the Nahlim Forest are one thing, but the chiefs are another. Many profit secretly from their shamans, and will be loath to turn on the source of their ill-gotten wealth."

20. A Poisoned Blade

Shar considered what to do. The Silent Owl Clan seemed as likely a candidate as any other for her next attempt at growing her army. The chiefs, who knew a great deal more about them than Shar did, were not overly hopeful of persuading their leader to join them though.

"We will do this," she said. "Nogrod, you will gather such an army as you can from your people. Maklar is already doing so. We'll join those forces together and march toward the Silent Owls."

"In winter, Nakatath?"

"It isn't winter yet, my friend."

"But it will be soon."

"That's so. And I know the tribes don't fight in winter. But pay heed, neither do they join together in cooperation or occupy a fortress. The tribes in the east have done so under my leadership. They have changed their ways, and they know now those changes keep them alive. They *like* them now."

"It may be, also," added Maklar, "that the shamans will drive the Nagraks to war against us over winter as well. If we aren't prepared for that, then they might crush us before our own rebellion has even gotten underway."

Nogrod ran a hand through his black hair. "So be it. Change is coming, and it's better to ride it than be trampled beneath it as it passes."

Another fish jumped in the lake, unseen, and the cold stars glittered in the deepening night.

"Will you make war on the Silent Owls and force them to join us?" Nogrod asked.

"Not if I can help it. We'll send messages of friendship before us, and tell them that the rebellion is begun. The army will only be there to persuade the chief to join us."

"And if he does not?" Maklar asked.

"Then the army is still a last resort. The warriors of the Silent Owl Clan may take matters into their own hands, and force their chief to join us, or replace him."

They passed that night, and another by the lake. All the while messengers ran to and fro, and Nogrod gathered his army together and organized supplies. He was not as skilled as Maklar at logistics, but the two of them worked well together, and Maklar offered much support.

Messengers went also back to the Roaring Stags, and the two forces came together and headed south toward Silent Owl territory.

It was not a great army. It was smaller by far than the one Shar had built before, but she was pleased nevertheless. There were nearly three thousand men here, and it was a force to be reckoned with. It was the beginning of something bigger, and even the greatest trees grew from a small nut. If she had but time, it would swell as word raged through Nahlim Forest.

Word *would* be spreading. She could hope that other clans would join her of their own accord, yet there was a danger in that too. The shamans, and whatever other enemies she had in the forest, knew of her presence now and they would be taking what steps they could against her.

Shar led the army, and she set a grueling pace. The men did not grumble at that, for she walked on her own two feet and disdained the pony that was offered to her. What she could do, the men were determined to match.

They encamped at dusk, and Shar was tired. Even so, she moved around the camp speaking with as many as she could and sharing a few jokes by their cooking fires while they ate, and then late into the night while they told stories. Radatan, Huigar and Asana were always with her, acting as guards. She had not forgotten the ten thousand in gold the shamans had put on her head. Even Boldgrim came with her, for the Leaping Deer shaman had not been seen, and no one knew where he was. He could be in the camp, hidden, and planning an attack.

They set off at first light next day. The sky was dim with a cover of rolling clouds that brought no rain. It was good marching weather though, for it was neither hot nor cold. However, the mosquitoes that lived in abundance in this wetter part of the forest became a nuisance, and while the army traveled there were no smoky campfires to drive them away.

The forest began to change. The trees thickened, and it grew dark under their canopy. The beech trees gave way to other varieties, often black willows, aspen and birch, along with several kinds that Shar did not know. The earth grew wet and damp, and often the army traversed boggy patches and crossed fern-choked ravines.

It was in such a place, later in the day, that the ordinary routine of marching was abruptly broken. Shouts came from the left of Shar, and despite the scouts that had been sent ahead a group of attackers, perhaps twenty strong, burst from out of the ferns and swept forward.

They did not come for the army. They were too few. They came for Shar, and she drew her swords even as her guards stepped before her.

Radatan killed a man, and Huigar two. Quickly, the men around Shar leaped to defend her as well, and in moments the attackers were outnumbered. Yet one of them, his head hooded and no sword in his hand, suddenly threw a knife. It came for Shar through a gap in the defenders. Asana struck at it with his sword, but missed and it plunged toward Shar. She dodged out of the way, but did not see until too late the second figure, hooded and swordless like the first, that cast another blade. This struck her shoulder, cut through the cloth of her cloak and bit into her flesh.

The attackers fled then, disappearing among the ferns. A chase was made, and some of the enemy killed. For the most part, they vanished though, and the pursuit faltered.

Asana approached. "Are you hurt?"

Shar had barely felt it at the time, but it throbbed now and she moved her arm tenderly.

"It's nothing. A scratch only."

Asana looked thoughtful, and his gaze looked absently into the shadows of the gulley.

"Perhaps. And yet this is strange. Those attackers came for you, and they fled the moment you were struck. Perhaps they were merely scared away…"

"Or?"

"Or perhaps the blade was poisoned and they thought their work was done."

That sent a shiver up Shar's spine. She looked for the knife, and found it nearby on the ground.

"Do not touch it," Boldgrim said.

Shar had not seen the Nahat approach, but she was glad he was there. He picked up the blade himself, yet he used a piece of cloth to do so. There was blood and dirt on it, but he sniffed it several times.

"I can't detect any poison," he said, but he kept looking at it, frowning.

Maklar came close and studied it too. "It's a knife such as the Silent Owls use. And the men we killed were Silent Owls too. It might be that their chief sent them."

That was not good news, but Shar was not convinced either.

"Perhaps. Time will tell on that. It seems likely to me that it was shamans' work, and the Leaping Deer shaman is still missing. Where else would he go but to help, or seek help from, the shaman of a nearby tribe? Anyway, let's go forward. Time presses."

Boldgrim's frown deepened. "Wait," he said.

Shar was impatient to get moving again, yet Boldgrim had earned her trust. She could see no reason for delay, but if he wanted it, he would get it.

Slowly the shaman passed his hand over the blade. Nothing happened. He did so again, muttering some incantation. Again, nothing happened.

Shar studied the shaman. He looked concerned, and despite the fact that the knife was just a knife, and that he could detect no poison, she grew concerned herself. Maybe it was anxiety, but she began to feel unwell.

"Build a fire," Boldgrim commanded. "Swiftly."

The others hesitated, wanting just as Shar did to be moving again and to get out of this part of the forest where they had been attacked. Even so, Shar gave a gesture indicating assent, and they then moved quickly to do as the shaman asked.

A fire was soon roaring to life, and it was smoky for much of the material was damp. Yet still there were several logs that, once having caught fire properly, began to burn with great heat.

Boldgrim knelt down close, and he reached in quickly to place the knife on one of the logs. The hilt was made of some kind of bone, and it blackened but did not burn. The blade, however, melted swiftly and the liquid metal hissed and bubbled, causing the fire to crack and pop as it reached upward with twirling tendrils.

"Strange," Radatan said. "I've never seen metal melt like that. The blade should be unharmed in a fire. Even in a forge, it should merely have glowed red hot."

"That is because it is no ordinary knife," Boldgrim said, standing. "Sorcery has been worked upon it. Powerful sorcery, too strong for the metal to endure, and in its weakened state only a little heat was needed to destroy it."

"What kind of sorcery?" Shar asked. "I begin to feel unwell."

The sharp eyes of Boldgrim studied her. "Death sorcery. It is a wicked magic, more the province of witches than shamans, though few have the power to practice it."

Boldgrim gave her little hope, but he took command and started giving orders.

"The army must camp here," he said. "We will be going nowhere for a while. And build up this fire more and get some water boiling."

Shar began to shiver, and though the dusk was approaching, she felt a darkness creep over her eyes that surely was not the lowering sun.

"Is there some herb that might combat what the knife has done?" she asked.

Boldgrim led her to sit down beside the fire. "It is no poison that can be remedied with a herb or the like. It is magic. And it needs magic to fight it. Well for you that I discovered this so soon. The longer the sorcery has to take hold the harder it is to defeat." He looked at her earnestly. "I will not lie though. I have only heard of this, and never seen it. In all the examples I have heard though, the patient died."

"It will be what it will be," Shar said. "I've given everything to the cause, and if it isn't enough, it isn't enough."

Boldgrim lifted her cloak off her shoulder and pulled aside the top of her tunic to expose the wound. Shar let him do what he needed without comment, and beckoned Asana over. The swordmaster stood nearby, his face pale and his expression as of stone.

"If I die," she said, "then—"

"You will not," he interrupted. "The Cheng people need you. The rebellion needs you."

"Need and reality aren't the same thing. I may die. I have known the risk since my youth, and it was brought home to me as a palpable truth the first day we met. I have had great luck to survive this long. But if my luck is over, then I have a final ... wish." She had almost said command, but this was something that could not be ordered.

"Speak on," Asana said quietly. "It will be fulfilled."

"I want you to take my place. It's almost a death sentence, but the Cheng people need it. Take my place, and become the figurehead of the rebellion. Only you have a chance of doing it. You're respected throughout the land. Revered. Only you might unite the tribes as I have tried to do."

Asana bowed his head. "You will lead them yourself. Yet if the worst should happen, then I will try to lead in your place, in honor of your memory."

Shar placed a hand over his. "It's a great burden. I'm sorry. You'll curse me when that begins to dawn on you. But it's not about me, or you. It's about the people of the land who need someone to fight against the shamans. Someone to show them the way."

Boldgrim began to chant louder, and a strange light played over the tips of his fingers. Shar could see a dark tinge to her flesh beneath them, growing. It was like a bruise, only a cold crept with it and she felt her arm begin to grow numb, and her vision darkened more.

"Are you there, Maklar and Nogrod?"

"We are here, Nakatath."

It was the old man who answered, but she could barely see him now. Maybe she had passed out and night had come. She did not like to think of the alternative.

"Will the both of you follow Asana? Will you obey him as you obey me? Do you recognize that if you don't, the rebellion will collapse and the shamans might become even worse tyrants, and dominate the people for another thousand years?"

They hesitated. As well they might, for Shar Fei was the prophecy and Asana was not. She had the violet eyes and the twin swords, and Asana did not. At the same time though, not to go on was to die, for the shamans would ensure their killing if the rebellion failed. And Asana was *Asana*, famed in every clan.

"I will follow him," Maklar said.

"As will I," Nogrod repeated.

Shar was not sure if she heard them properly. The dark swelled around her, and she could not believe how swiftly the magic in the knife had overcome her.

The dark was deep, and her hearing was dim. Boldgrim still chanted, but at times that faded. Then there were drums beating in the distance. Or perhaps it was the slow thud of her own heart.

Shar Fei, a voice said. *You must not die.*

Shar Fei, another voiced added. *You must live.*

She could not tell where the voices came from. It was not Boldgrim. They said other things to her, but she drifted on a wave of oblivion and did not hear. At least her conscious mind.

Was she going mad? Her heart beat louder at that thought.

You are not mad, Shar Fei. You are strong. You will live. We require it.

Her shoulder throbbed, and she felt the coldness of it reaching to the rest of her body. Then there was an ache at her hips, and a warmth that spread outward to fight against the cold. It was the Swords of Dawn and Dusk.

She felt them come alive with magic as they touched her body, and Boldgrim's chanting faltered momentarily.

It is not your time, Shar Fei. And we thirst for blood and chaos. Only you can give us that. Live, and be strong!

It was the demons in the blade talking to her. Or madness. She was not sure, and at last all faded and the blackness swallowed her mind.

Time passed. Eons came and went, or the hundredth part of a single moment. Oblivion rendered time meaningless, and Shar rode on a wave of forgetfulness so deep that all troubles, fear, joy or yearnings were not even shadows of shadows.

Yet a light came to her, and her mind blossomed into it. She remembered, and she knew her destiny. The light was not of the swords, nor of the void. Nor was it from herself or Boldgrim. It merely was, and all the universe was in it.

It was dawn. Shar woke, and she felt refreshed. Boldgrim was beside her, sitting with his back to a fire that had burned to embers. The others were there too, asleep. Yet all around her the army was bustling. No doubt her friends had stayed awake late into the night out of concern for her.

She sat up. Her shoulder was a little stiff, but that was all. Once more she had escaped death, and once more the shamans had failed to kill her. They might, one day. But not yet. She had too much to do.

"Time to be up and moving," she said.

Boldgrim was the first to react. He had not been asleep, but merely resting.

"Lady," he said. "You have the luck of the gods. Or something else." His gaze flickered to her swords, and she knew he had perceived the demons, and she remembered herself what they had said and knew it was not a dream brought on by fever.

The others took turns to hug her, and she grew embarrassed. She did not like being the center of attention, but it soon grew worse.

A soldier nearby saw her, and he cried out. "She lives!"

The call was taken up by others round about, and soon the whole army was shouting and cheering.

Shar drew a sword and cast it up into the air, catching it by the hilt as it arced down, and then swept forward in a bow to the army. They cheered even louder.

"Forget about being an emperor," Radatan said. "You should have been a gleeman."

The army marched again, and much to Shar's chagrin she now rode a pony. She was still weak, but she was alive, and she thanked Boldgrim deeply.

"It might have been my magic," he said. "Maybe. It played a part anyway." He said no more, and he looked as one in deep thought as they progressed through the forest and into flatter and more open lands.

By midafternoon, Shar dismounted. She was feeling better, and just as importantly, she did not wish to appear weak when she met Silent Owl warriors, which must happen soon now. They had entered their lands, and no doubt word of their coming had long preceded them.

It happened sooner than she thought. The chief himself approached through the forest, a hundred warriors around him. He was middle aged, tending to a round belly and he rode a fat pony.

They met in a clearing, a hundred of Shar's army coming forward with her as her own guard.

"Why do you bring an army against me?" the chief asked bluntly.

Shar gazed at him coldly, letting her violet eyes intimidate him. He tried not to look away, but then glanced at his boots. She chose that moment to reply.

"Against you? You are mistaken, O chief. This army has one true enemy. That is not any Cheng tribe, but the shamans. You have heard, have you not, that a rebellion is underway?"

"So I have heard."

Shar did not like him. She did not trust him. And he may have sought her death, or known the attempt would be made. Or not. She had no way of knowing for sure. It was time to put him under stress though. That was always the way to discover what a person was made of.

"I lead that rebellion. The shamans would dearly like to kill me. They have tried many times, including yesterday with a magic-touched blade. It was cast by a Silent Owl. Do you know anything about that?"

The chief's face was blank. He showed nothing of what he thought, which indicated to Shar that he had known of the attempt. A more normal reaction would have been surprise or concern. Still, she could not be certain.

The chief turned around and beckoned someone to come up from his group. Not all of them were warriors, for the man who approached, old and white haired, was a shaman. He had concealed himself with a hood, but now he threw it back proudly.

"Svathkin, you stand accused of an assassination attempt. What say you."

The shaman grinned at Shar, and there was malice in his eyes.

"I know nothing of it, but there is a price on your head. Ten thousand in gold to whomever kills you. I would gladly pay it."

Shar felt her anger rise, but she ignored it. So too she ignored the shaman.

"O chief, who rules the Silent Owls? Do they take orders from you, or are they the slave dogs of the shamans?"

"I am chief. I rule."

She could see anger in the chief's eyes, and she liked that. He was under the thumb of the shamans, but at least part of him did not like it. It was time to bring all this to a head.

"Then join me. This army at my back isn't here to go against you. It's here to support you against the child killers that are the shamans. Against the tyrants that sow discord over the land so they can divide and rule. It is against those who gather wealth to themselves while the tribes live in poverty."

The shaman hissed. Shar ignored him, and kept her eyes fixed on the chief. Yet she held her hands close to the hilts of her swords, and her friends were close to her, ready to act the moment any hostility broke out.

Without doubt, the shaman knew he was a dead man if he tried anything. He did not move, but seethed in impotent fury. The chief squirmed too. He wanted support from the shaman, but none was coming. He, at the very least, guessed the accusations against the shamans were true, but he benefited from them so he did not like to call them out, but nor could he deny what had been said without looking like a liar before his men.

He took the politician's approach, which was to obfuscate.

"You have said much, and given me pause for thought. This is too great a matter to decide now. It needs deliberation among my elders. I will think on it, and get back to you in due course. In the meantime, I expect you to keep your army clear of my lands. If you come any closer, we must regard it as an act of war."

Shar smiled at him. Better to make him think she knew something he did not than to show her displeasure.

"We are at war, chief. The rebellion moves on apace, and I cannot say where or when this army will move. Make haste, and decide quickly."

The chief left then, taking his retinue with him. Only the shaman looked back, and his glance darted venom.

21. The Game of Nobility

Shar's army established a camp, and she set several strong rings of sentries and instructed the scouts to patrol ceaselessly through the night. She did not believe in the Silent Owl chief, and still less did she trust his shaman.

After dinner, Shar sat by the smoky fire with Maklar, Nogrod, and her own advisors.

"What do you think the Silent Owls will do?" she asked.

Maklar shook his head. "I'm disappointed in them. Or at least their chief. I think this is nothing more than a delaying tactic. He'll not join you."

"A delaying tactic for what purpose?" Shar already knew the answer. She wanted to test her own reasoning against that of others.

"For one purpose, and one alone," Asana answered. "They'll have sent word to the shamans for help. By force of arms, or by sorcery, they intend to destroy you here. Your army is much smaller in this forest than in Chatchek Fortress, and that makes you more vulnerable. This chief and his shaman will do anything, and say anything, just to delay you until the shamans can act against you."

Shar glanced at the others. "Your opinion?"

No one disagreed. It was obvious, but at the same time Shar was in a difficult situation.

"I could force the issue," she said. "Tomorrow I could march into Silent Owl territory, and see if the tribe is behind their chief and shaman. They may not fight for them, and instead welcome me."

Nogrod fed some timber into the fire. "I think they would support you. At the least, half their tribe would hold back. They may even fight each other."

Shar pulled her cloak tighter about her. Despite the fire, the night brought with it a growing cold.

"That's likely true. But then the shamans can paint a picture of me as a warmonger who brings chaos in her wake, and stirs the tribes to spill their own blood. It'll be harder for me to get other tribes to join the cause, then."

They considered that, and no one liked it. It was close to the truth. She *did* bring war and chaos. It was for a purpose, and a noble one at that, but people bled just the same whether the purpose was noble or infamous. The best lies were always based on truth, and this was a little too close to the truth. A twist here, or there, and she could be seen as the tyrant and the shamans as protectors.

Other ways existed though. Other choices could be made. Politics, war and diplomacy were all the same thing. All that changed was the tactics, and that was what made them look different. At heart, they were not.

"Does the Silent Owl chief have a rival?"

Asana was the first to react to that. She saw him nod almost imperceptibly to himself. He understood the direction this question was headed, but the others would not be far behind him.

"He has a young cousin called Dastrin," Maklar said. "A popular man, and brave. He's said to hunt wild boar with a spear, which is a dangerous pursuit much admired in the forest for its bravery. But the chief, angry with him at some exchange of words, demoted him from his position as leader of a band of warriors. The band of warriors would not accept the new leader the chief appointed though. Since then, there's been tension between them. The chief would like to arrest his cousin and the band of warriors, but fears an outcry if he does." Maklar paused. "So rumor says, anyway."

Shar was a little surprised. News traveled fast in the forest tribes, and she sensed they were not as hostile to each other as many other tribes through the old Cheng Empire. The shamans seemed to have a little less control too. Likely all this was because the forest tribes were relatively few in number, and the shamans did not fear an uprising from them as much as many other tribes. The Nagraks, the largest tribe by far, were the most supportive of the shamans. The tribe's children were compulsorily indoctrinated into the approved belief systems the moment they reached speaking age.

Shar waved some smoke away from her face, and her shoulder throbbed a little. She was still not fully recovered from the attempt on her life, but she ignored it.

"I don't think we have much time to spare. The Silent Owls aren't going to be allowed to cooperate, even if the bulk of them want to, and the longer we delay, the more danger we're in. I'm going to send word to this cousin, and promise him the chieftainship if he tries to overthrow the chief. If he succeeds, all is well. If he looks like he might fail, I can step in before that with military aid under a pretext of preventing further bloodshed."

"It might work," Nogrod said. "It just might. And it could all happen quickly too."

Maklar was not as convinced. "The idea might work. It relies on getting a message of support and encouragement through to Dastrin though. But if we can think of a plan like that, the enemy will too. They'll be having any of their likely rebels watched, and the forest will be alive with scouts making sure no attack, or message, gets through undetected."

Shar liked the way he thought. He was completely right, but he did not know all that she did. He did not know, nor guess, that Boldgrim could pass through unhindered merely by pretending to be a shaman from the Nagraks. And if he were accosted, he had the power to defend himself.

She glanced at the Nahat, and he, reading her intention, nodded agreement.

"Boldgrim can undertake the mission. He'll pass through whatever net of scouts is thrown up against him. He will carry the message where it is intended, and he will return to bring us a reply."

Some of them did not seem so sure of this plan, but they did not know Boldgrim like she did. She beckoned him over.

"Best to leave now," she said. "Time, as ever, is our enemy."

"I will, milady, but I do not like to leave you unguarded. What if the shamans attack you while I am away?"

"All choices carry their risks," she said. "And thank you for thinking of it. But that danger will only increase as the days pass. The sooner you go, the sooner you can return." She smiled at him and patted her sword hilts. "Besides, I'm not without protection that even the shamans fear."

Boldgrim made ready then, getting some specific directions from Maklar as to where this Dastrin would most likely be found, but before he left Shar beckoned him over and whispered something in his ear.

Then the shaman was gone, blending swiftly and silently into the night forest. She did not fear for him. The enemy would not see him, and if they did they would take him for a shaman, or a nazram, or a warrior. A bit of magic went a long way, and the forest was too vast to guard every path.

They talked into the night, discussing what was likely to happen and making plans for the future. One way or the other, Shar would have the Silent Owls as part of her army, and then the other tribes, seeing the growth of her force, would be more likely to join her. She could not account for what the shamans might do though. They held great power, and the more she pushed them the more desperate they would get. They might use it.

They waited, and the night was uneventful except that several Silent Owl scouts were observed by Shar's own. Under her instructions, they were not killed but merely turned around and sent away. She was not at war with the Silent Owls, and wished no bad blood between their forces and hers. Better that Dastrin started that.

The next day brought no change. It was too soon, but perhaps by evening Boldgrim might return. To fill in their time, Shar had the army complete several maneuvers, practicing how they moved as a single unit and trying to break down the natural distrust between tribes. They formed squares, trained using archers at the front of a line who were then absorbed back into the army as lines of spear and swordsmen came to the front. And messengers were chosen and signals for various actions decided upon, mostly by horn but also by flag. These Shar ensured matched her army back in Chatchek Fortress. If they ever fought together, that would be necessary.

The chiefs occupied much of their time asking her questions about what was happening in the east. She gave them accounts of her battles, and the tactics she had used as well as those of the shamans.

Toward evening, they all grew more tense. Boldgrim could be expected back soon, but there was no sign of him as yet. The delay ate away at Shar too, for while her army was still the shamans might be moving, and it was impossible to say what they might do.

As the long rays of the westering sun slanted through the forest, and the cooking fires of her camp were starting to be lit, the sound of distant battle came to them dimly through the forest. What exactly it signified, Shar could not be sure until Boldgrim returned. And still, there was no sign of him even as the night closed in.

22. I Have Done It Before

Rumor of battle drifted down the shadowy aisles of the trees. Shar's army was roused, and she set them in a defensive square but made as yet no move to march.

The night was a bad time to fight, for it was hard to tell friend from foe. And she could not be sure if it were not a trap intended to get her to move in the dark, and then make her vulnerable to ambush.

She waited. The sounds of battle grew louder, and at times the ruddy flare of fire was seen in the distance. Nogrod wanted to march and help, for surely it must be the very rebellion in action that Shar herself had tried to foment. Maklar, wiser to the way of the world, agreed with Shar.

"Patience," the old man said. "Haste makes errors."

Shar's patience was rewarded. Out of the dark a cloaked figure approached. She nearly drew her swords, for there was a look of danger about him. Then she realized it was Boldgrim, returned at last.

"What news?" she asked.

"Good news, milady. I have spoken with Dastrin."

"And what reply does he give?"

"You hear it now. Battle is joined between his forces and the chief's."

"It was a quick decision, then."

"Quicker even than that. I found him already marching with his men. He seeks to surround the chief, and take him by surprise. There is resistance though, but as far as I can tell most warriors have taken no side. They don't like the chief. They don't want to rebel either. They merely wait to see who will win, and they will serve that person."

Shar thought quickly. "Good work. We must ensure Dastrin gains that victory, but not by dint of our army. We'll go in, but with only three hundred warriors. It's enough to make a difference, but not so many that anyone could say I invaded."

Shar gave swift orders, and the army further strengthened its sentries and established defensive lines against the possibility of attack. Yet she herself led out the three hundred men, a mixture of Roaring Stag and Leaping Deer warriors, into the forest and toward the sounds of battle.

Scouts were sent out, but Boldgrim was by her side and he knew where he was going. He had just come through this area.

The night was dark around them, and the dim sounds of battle were eerie within it. Lights flashed at times, and the smell of smoke was in the air. Huts were burning, and it was a terrible thing. So too the screams that occasionally rose up over the background noise to pierce the darkness with a chill.

Shar drew her swords. Huigar and Radatan were close by her side. Asana was nearby too, yet he walked calmly and had not yet drawn his blade. Boldgrim was at the head of the group, his staff in a ready position and his eyes searching the darkness.

It did not take long for the sounds of battle to increase. Soon they could see skirmishes by the ruddy glow of a burning hut, but the fight had moved beyond a village and into the forest behind it.

"This is the chief's village," Maklar said.

They went on, swinging around to the side. They could not be sure who was who in the dark, and soon the main battle was visible. Two forces struggled against each other, and Shar's scouts returned with word from Dastrin. He was on the left side, and he requested help.

Shar did not hesitate. She had promised help, and it would be given. Quickly she gave orders, and her force circled around to come up behind the chief.

The enemy was caught between two forces, but they did not surrender, nor were they beaten. They formed a line against Shar's men, and they held it against her attack.

Huigar and Radatan gave her reproachful looks, but Shar fought herself. It was not necessary from a military point of view, but that was not all she had her eye on. If she proved herself in battle here, as she had done in the east, it would help her gather the tribes to her banner. Word would spread about her skill and courage, and that was worth as much to her as twin swords or violet eyes.

A huge man came at her, thrusting a long spear forward from the enemy line. It nearly impaled her, but she dodged the deadly tip and then broke the shaft with a downward strike of her swords. Then, using one sword folded up inside her forearm as a shield to protect herself, she darted in and slit his throat with the tip of her other sword.

The enemy line began to weaken. The chief's force was outnumbered, and now the descendant of Chen Fei came at them herself with fiery eyes.

A little longer the battle lasted, then men started throwing down their weapons and surrendering. These were quickly rounded up and taken prisoner, but a smaller group in the center had not yet given up. They fought futilely, but with valor. They were nazram, but Shar did not hold that against them.

The small force was soon surrounded, and still they fought on. A man called out to them, and he spoke with authority.

"Throw down your weapons!" he ordered. "Dying will not help the Cheng people. Surrender, live, and serve your nation another day."

"Keep fighting!" replied a voice from the midst of the enemy. Dawn was at hand now. And in the dim light Shar thought she could make out the chief urging the nazram on.

The nazram had courage, but they were not stupid. They fought a little longer, but then surrendered despite the urgings of their chief. They were led away to where the rest of their force was being held, and disarmed, the chief yelling and screaming all the way. It would do him no good, and by contrast Dastrin was calm in victory and not vengeful.

"You are the new chief," Shar said when they met.

"And you are Nakatath, and my sword is at your service."

He went on then to give instructions to his men, one of which was to announce that he had taken over the role of leader of the Silent Owls, and that the tribe supported Shar Fei.

"So much for the old chief," Radatan said. "But what of the shaman?"

"I know his kind," Maklar answered. "He'll be long gone now."

"Perhaps. But I suspect not," Shar said. "At any rate, it's time to find out. Where is his hut?"

"Near the old chief's, back in the village," Maklar told her.

Shar gathered her men about her, and they hastened to the village. They entered it, noting that many of the inhabitants, older men, women and children, came out to cheer Shar as she walked through.

They soon came to the village center, and there they found a hut, ringed by warriors. There were signs of battle here, for the bodies of several nazram lay outside, killed in a quick fight.

"There must be more inside," Maklar said, "but the shaman would have long since fled."

"I don't think so," Shar replied, drawing her swords.

So it proved. As they came up one of the warriors broke from the ring and bowed to Shar Fei.

"Nakatath, all has been done as you requested through Chief Dastrin. We laid in wait until the shaman and his men came. Even as you guessed, they tried to recover something from the hut and flee, but we have not let them."

"Good work," Shar answered. "We'll see soon what the shaman wanted to take away."

Shar went to the hut and called out. "Nazram! If you put down your swords and come out, you will leave as free men. But the shaman is accused of crimes against the Cheng Empire, and he will face my judgement. For I am Shar Fei, descendent of Chen Fei, and I am the emperor-to-be."

She said no more. From inside there was a mutter of voices. The sun rose higher over the rim of the world, and it was red in the smoke-ridden air.

"And if we don't come out?" a voice called.

"Then the hut will be burned, with you in it."

There was silence for a while, and Dastrin himself arrived. Then one at a time, the nazram exited the hut. The shaman came last, and he looked wrathful as a storm cloud. His eyes seemed to pop from his red face, and his hands trembled. Not with fear, but anger.

Even so, he made no attempt to use magic. Not yet, anyway. He knew the moment he tried that arrow and spear would strike at him, and if not them the two swords of Shar Fei that he eyed with fear would seek his life.

"What do we do with him?" Dastrin asked Shar.

"Let me question him first, and see if he repents. Then what must be must be."

23. A Ghostly Image

Shar daunted the shaman with her violet eyes. She could read his fear, for he knew that his life was at risk and the rule of the shamans was vulnerable.

"Tell me truthfully, O shaman," she asked. "Have you contacted your brethren and asked for help?"

A moment he looked at her in silence, and she did not think he would reply. Then he answered in a surly voice, but he had mastered his fear and spoke with boldness.

"Of course. They're coming for you, Shar Fei. And you will die. If you think this is a victory, you are mistaken. It is the beginning of the end."

She did not sheath her swords. There was venom in his voice, and he might yet attack her.

"I say the same to you, shaman. It's the beginning of the end for the rule of your order. Your time is done. You, however, need not die. Do you acknowledge your tyranny? Do you repent of it?"

"No."

Shar signaled Radatan over. "Go inside the hut. Search for any hidden treasure trove, and bring out whatever you find."

There was silence while they waited. The shaman stood still, disdaining to look at Shar. She, for her part, did not take her eyes off him. He was still a threat, and he had magic to help him escape, or to try to kill her.

Radatan came back quickly. He carried a chest some two feet long by a foot high and wide.

"This was on a table inside. It looks like it was dug up from beneath the floor of the hut."

He pulled open the lid, and ran his hand through a pile of gold coins, letting them drip back into the box like a flow of water. Then he did the same with necklaces of bright jewels and gleaming bracelets. There was a fortune in the box.

"The wealth of the Cheng people, stolen over the years." Shar said. "Meanwhile we live in poverty. Do you know any shame, tyrant?"

With a proud glance, the shaman ignored her. Or so it seemed. Yet this was a guise, for he raised his hands and fire flared at his fingertips. He made to cast some sorcery at Shar.

He did not get far. Faster than Shar even, who was raising her blades, Huigar hurled a knife that she must have had ready in her hand. It streaked through the air, a glittering arc of death, and took the shaman in the throat.

The fire died on his hands. He fell, blood spurting from his neck. A moment longer he lived, eyes blazing with hatred, and then he died.

"What have you done?" Dastrin asked, turning to Huigar. "It's forbidden to kill a shaman."

"She has done her job and protected me." Shar answered. "The *shamans* say it is forbidden to kill a shaman. Well, they would. But they bleed like all others. I know, for I've killed my share."

It would take a long time to undo the teachings of the shamans, even when they were overthrown and cast out. Greedy tyrants they might be, but they were not stupid. They spent much time and effort indoctrinating youth into their way of thinking. The evil they begot would live after their deaths.

Shar had not forgotten that the shaman had admitted sending for help. Probably it was already on the way, even before then, and she must act swiftly now. Doing the unexpected would be an asset, and she must give that thought.

She held a meeting with Dastrin. "You are chief of the Silent Owls now," she said. "And the Roaring Stags and Leaping Deer are your friends. Trust in them, and they will trust in you. Learn to think in new ways, and to cast off the dictates of the shamans."

"You speak as one who will not be here?"

Shar hesitated. This was a difficult decision. "I won't be. You can see now how the tribes can act together. Take Maklar for your leader, as he is old and wise. Together, you can do anything. But I will return."

Dastrin nodded gravely. "It's not easy, but you're right. Where will you go?"

This, Shar was not prepared to say publicly. There was a price on her head, after all, and the shamans sought to kill her.

"I go to bring you other help. You, Maklar and Nogrod must travel through the forest and rouse the remaining tribes. It will be much easier now, for you are already three banded together. It's an example to the others, and you'll find that most tribes are eager to cast down the shamans who try to control their lives. Be fair and calm. Inspire trust. Show the enemy are vulnerable. The forest tribes will flock to you."

Shar said swift goodbyes then to the other chiefs, laid out her plan for their progress through the forest, and obtained assurances they would follow Maklar's lead. Yet well before dusk, she was on her way again with just her own companions.

"Where do we go?" Asana asked.

"To the Skultic Mountains. They're only a hundred or so miles from where we are. Probably less."

"I thought as much," Asana replied. "You want to reach there before winter sets in and travel becomes too difficult."

Shar realized, not for the first time, what a great strategist Asana was. He could tell what she was going to do often before she did it. If the enemy had someone like that, it would cause her great trouble. So far, at least, whoever commanded them did not have such insights though.

The chiefs gave them all the supplies they needed, and Shar and her companions once more walked by themselves. They had the passwords that were in use between the forest tribes now though, so if they were discovered by scouts they could prove they were on the business of the chiefs, and should be unmolested. With luck though, no one would see them. The sooner they reached the mountains, and preferably without any detection of their movements, the better.

The forest changed little. Two days they passed through it, heading southeast. There were settlements and scouts, but they wove a way through without being seen. The trees ended abruptly early on the third day though.

They stood on grassland now, the forest behind them and ahead a rolling grassland. Beyond it, towering up into the sky was a mountain range.

"The Skultic Mountains," Asana said. "A dangerous place at any time of year, but worse in winter."

"You've been there?" Shar asked.

"I have, but it was long ago. It's scarcely populated on this side. But toward the middle are many fertile dales and larger settlements. It's not toward a settlement that you head though, is it?"

Again he had deduced her plan. It was almost annoying.

"No. Not at first. I'm heading for the Nashwan Temple."

"It still exists?" Boldgrim seemed surprised.

"It does. They're powerful, but many smaller temples have been destroyed by the shamans."

"What's this Nashwan Temple?" Radatan asked.

It was hard to describe, but Shar had Shulu's teachings to fall back on, and they could be comprehensive but terse at the same time.

"They're monks. They have no mystic power like shamans, though people often suspect them of it. They worship the gods, in their own way, and they pass on lore to the common people of the history of the immortal pantheon. But unlike others of their kind, they're fighting monks, greatly skilled in combat, with or without weapons. It's said they number three hundred, and that they are a match for an army of three thousand. So the story goes, anyway. But they have greater value than that to me. They're revered in the Skultic Mountains, and if they join me so will all the mountain tribes. And that's, perhaps, five thousand."

Radatan whistled. "Well, now your plan makes a lot more sense."

"You doubted me?" Shar asked with a grin.

"Maybe a little. I don't like you leaving those forest tribes to their own devices. But that Maklar has a wise old head on his shoulders, and I can see why you're coming here now. I'm sure it will all work out."

Shar was not so sure herself. So much could go wrong, and Shulu had said the Nashwan monks could be unpredictable. Still, it was the best plan she had and there was no alternative but to push forward with it.

For the next two days they pressed ahead, climbing ever upward over the rolling hills until they were in the mountains themselves.

It grew colder. The wind howled at whiles, and in the mornings, if the wind abated, frost slicked the ground. Eagles circled in the sky, but this was their territory and they showed no interest in the human travelers that toiled below them.

And toil it was, for the paths were steep and more suited to four-footed beasts than two-footed trespassers. Such the travelers felt, for this was a wild land without human occupation that they could see. There was no smoke, nor any herds of cattle, sheep or goats.

"Where is this Nashwan Temple?" Radatan asked. "Is there anything in this land but rock and open air?"

"It's close," Shar answered. "Shulu taught me the way, and barren as this place seems, they thrive here. Still, much of their food comes from the inner dales that are more fertile than here."

So it proved. Toward evening they came to a ridge, and climbing to its top they saw a dale before them. It was rocky and steep, yet on a strange hill that rose from the bottom was a kind of fortress. It stretched up elegantly to the sky, with towers and spires, yet it was encircled by a wall. One intended to keep enemies without.

They trudged toward it as night fell. They saw no one, yet a horn was blown and lights flared to life as torches were lit atop the walls and at the base where a great gate was set. It was smaller by far than Chatchek Fortress, and much more graceful. Even so, it would not be easy to take. Still less so for the men who lived here were warriors of great skill. Their brethren that once dwelled in many places across the land had fallen to time and shamanistic intrigues, but this fortress was still strong.

They came to the gate. It was open, but still they saw no one. Yet from the shadows a voice spoke.

"Welcome to the Nashwan temple, Shar Fei, descendant of Chen Fei, and scourge of the shamans."

The speaker stepped into the flickering light of a torch. He was a young man, and despite the cold he wore only a simple tunic without a cloak.

Shar inclined her head. "Thank you for the welcome. I would speak with your abbot."

"He is expecting you. Please follow me."

The monk did not move straight away. Instead, he glanced to Shar's side.

"Greetings to you too, Asana."

The swordmaster offered the warrior's salute, the right hand clenched in a fist symbolizing battle, and the open left palm meeting it, symbolizing peace.

No more was said. The young man led them through the gate tunnel, and into the courtyard beyond. Here were scores of men practicing martial pursuits. Some trained with swords, others axes or spears and a few weapons that Shar had never even seen before. Others sparred barehanded. Quite a few were doing exercises, stretches or meditating. It was a strange sight, and Shar gazed around with interest.

The courtyard was large, but eventually they reached a doorway to the inner keep. Here they entered, and the corridor was well lit by torches. From somewhere came the sound of chanting, but Shar could not identify its origin. At one moment it seemed to come from the left, and in the next from the right. It was a maze of corridors, but the young monk led them with calm assurance, picking a path without hesitation.

There were less corridors as they began to climb a flight of stairs. Higher and higher they went, and the chanting receded to a distant hum. Even that stopped as a gong was sounded, and the travelers were led into a single and narrow tower where the stairs spiraled higher and higher in an unbroken flight.

They came to the top, and their guide led them to an oak door, bound by iron.

"The abbot awaits you within," the guide said, and he left.

Radatan was about to knock on the door, but Asana stopped him.

"Wait a moment," the swordmaster said. "The abbot is coming."

"How can he know we are here?"

"He knows."

Even as Asana spoke, the door opened and a young boy beckoned them in, then he too departed.

Asana led them into the room at the top of the tower. It was a small room, but the windows were many and they offered a great view of the nighttime sky. A round table was at the center, and there the abbot sat. He was not eating, but several platters covered the table, and apart from his plate there were five others. Shar counted them again, and wondered if the abbot knew the number of the travelers that were coming to him, or if that were a coincidence.

"Welcome to the Nashwan Temple, Shar Fei. Welcome also Boldgrim, Huigar and Radatan. And welcome back, Asana. A long time it has been since last you stood here."

Asana bowed. "I hope I am wiser now than I was then, Master Kaan."

The abbot smiled. He was an ancient man, and his wispy hair was silver as frost.

"Wisdom is a path, my son. The journey counts for all. When one arrives at a destination, then their name is fool, for enlightenment has no end."

The old abbot glanced at Shar. "Forgive me, but Asana is an old student. Did he tell you that?"

Shar shook her head.

"No matter. Few of those who train here reveal it to the outside world. It is like a dream when you leave, is it not, Asana?"

"What is dream, and what is reality?" countered the swordmaster. "Perception is everything, but perception is full of falsehoods. The water that looks deep can be shallow, and the mind that can encompass the secrets of the world can forget what it is to love."

The old man clapped. "You always were a good student. But enough. We can talk of old times together later. For now, let us eat."

The abbot said a prayer, though to which of the gods it was directed to, or all of them, Shar was not sure. He spoke in a dialect that was difficult for her to understand, and she realized that the language must have been as it was long ago. Yet when not in prayer, he spoke the Cheng language as others did across the current day tribes.

The food was simple, but nourishing and tasty. There was no meat, but there were several dishes of a hearty nature, and others that were spicy. It was different from what Shar was used to, but she liked it.

They finished the meal and drank from a pot that contained heated water infused with herbs. From somewhere below, the gong sounded again and there was a fleeting sound of hymns being chanted, but then they faded away.

It was time to broach the reason for Shar's arrival, but she was not sure how to do it. The old man seemed kindly, but whether or not he was disposed to aid her, she could not tell.

"Do you know why I have come?" she asked the abbot.

"Of course," he replied. "You wish the aid of this monastery, first for our fighting ability, and secondly to inspire the tribes of these mountains to join you."

The old man was shrewd, and Shar liked him. If he had been a teacher of Asana, it was no surprise how the swordmaster had turned out.

"That saves me explaining things then," Shar replied. "All that remains is the answer you will give."

The abbot shook his head sadly. "Not all. But come, eat. Enjoy yourselves while you may. There will be time to ask questions and give answers after."

They ate in silence then, and the mood was broken. A deep gloom filled the chamber as though it reflected the mood of the abbot. Asana seemed thoughtful, and he glanced often at his old master as if trying to divine his thoughts, but he only looked more and more puzzled.

The gong rang again, and the abbot tilted his head as though listening. Chanting could be heard once more, and then it broke off suddenly.

"It begins," the abbot said.

"What begins, old friend?" Asana asked.

"Never mind. What must be must be. Just remember that the root of evil has its first growth in good, and that without the dark there is no light."

Shar did not know what he was talking about. They seemed old platitudes to her, but Asana began to turn pale.

"Even here, master?"

The old man was about to answer, but then the door was thrust open behind them. The young boy they had seen earlier returned, breathless.

"Master Kaan!"

"Be calm, my child," the old man said. "In haste, or in the turmoil of emotion, warriors make mistakes. True men face the storm with tranquility."

The boy tried to gather himself, but his anxiety still came through.

"Master Kaan, there is rebellion. Half the temple fights with the other half."

"And who leads the rebellion?"

"Master Bai-Mai. He says that the woman known as Shar Fei is worth ten thousand in gold. With that money we can start new temples to replace the ones that were lost, and that by giving her to the shamans we can secure our future. The shamans will treat us as allies and stop persecuting us."

Shar felt a chill deep in her bones. She had brought this on. She had not intended to, but it was a consequence of her being here. Men, once more, were dying for her. And if the abbot turned on her, all was lost. The Cheng Empire was slipping through her fingers, and her luck was running out. Perhaps, if Boldgrim opened a gate they might escape.

She glanced at the abbot. He gave no sign that he would acquiesce to the wishes of this Bai-Mai. If so, that made matters even worse. Could she abandon this temple to the chaos she had visited upon them, and just escape? She could not. But if she stayed, she would be given to the shamans.

Thus ends *Swords of Wrath*. The Shaman's Sword series continues in book six, *Swords of Fire*, where Shar's quest faces the resistance of men, magic and demons…

SWORDS OF FIRE

BOOK SIX OF THE SHAMAN'S SWORD SERIES

COMING SOON!

Amazon lists millions of titles, and I'm glad you discovered this one. But if you'd like to know when I release a new book, instead of leaving it to chance, sign up for my new release list. I'll send you an email on publication.

Yes please! – Go to www.homeofhighfantasy.com and sign up.

No thanks – I'll take my chances.

Dedication

There's a growing movement in fantasy literature. Its name is noblebright, and it's the opposite of grimdark.

Noblebright celebrates the virtues of heroism. It's an old-fashioned thing, as old as the first story ever told around a smoky campfire beneath ancient stars. It's storytelling that highlights courage and loyalty and hope for the spirit of humanity. It recognizes the dark, the dark in us all, and the dark in the villains of its stories. It recognizes death, and treachery and betrayal. But it dwells on none of these things.

I dedicate this book, such as it is, to that which is noblebright. And I thank the authors before me who held the torch high so that I could see the path: J.R.R. Tolkien, C.S. Lewis, Terry Brooks, Susan Cooper, Roger Taylor and many others. I salute you.

And, for a time, I too shall hold the torch high.

Appendix: Encyclopedic Glossary

Note: The history of the Cheng Empire is obscure, for the shamans hid much of it. Yet the truth was recorded in many places and passed down in family histories, in secret societies and especially among warrior culture. This glossary draws on much of that 'secret' history, and each book in this series is individualized to reflect the personal accounts that have come down through the dark tracts of time to the main actors within each book's pages. Additionally, there is often historical material provided in its entries for people, artifacts and events that are not included in the main text.

Many races dwell in Alithoras. All have their own language, and though sometimes related to one another the changes sparked by migration, isolation and various influences often render these tongues unintelligible to each other.

The ascendancy of Halathrin culture across the land, who are sometimes called elves, combined with their widespread efforts to secure and maintain allies against various evil incursions, has made their language the primary means of communication between diverse peoples. This was especially so during the Shadowed Wars, but has persisted through the centuries afterward.

This glossary contains a range of names and terms. Some are of Halathrin origin, and their meaning is provided.

The Cheng culture is also revered by its people, and many names are given in their tongue. It is important to remember that the empire was vast though, and there is no one Cheng language but rather a multitude of dialects. Perfect consistency of spelling and meaning is therefore not to be looked for.

List of abbreviations:

Cam. Camar

Chg. Cheng

Comb. Combined

Cor. Corrupted form

Hal. Halathrin

Prn. Pronounced

Ahat: *Chg.* "Hawk in the night." A special kind of assassin. Used by the shamans in particular, but open for hire to anybody who can afford their fee. It is said that the shamans subverted an entire tribe in the distant past, and that every member of the community, from the children to the elderly, train to hone their craft at killing and nothing else. They grow no crops, raise no livestock nor pursue any trade save the bringing of death. The fees of their assignments pay for all their needs. This is legend only, for no such community has ever been found. But the lands of the Cheng are wide and such a community, if it exists, would be hidden and guarded.

Alithoras: *Hal.* "Silver land." The Halathrin name for the continent they settled after leaving their own homeland. Refers to the extensive river and lake systems they found and their wonder at the beauty of the land.

Argash: *Chg.* "The clamor of war." Once a warrior of the Fen Wolf Tribe, and leader of a band of the leng-fah. Now chief of the clan.

Asana: *Chg.* "Gift of light." Rumored to be the greatest swordmaster in the history of the Cheng people. His father was a Duthenor tribesman from outside the bounds of the old Cheng Empire.

Bai-Mai: *Chg.* "Bushy eyebrows." One of the elders of the Nashwan Temple.

Boldgrim: A member of the Nahat.

Chen Fei: *Chg.* "Graceful swan." Swans are considered birds of wisdom and elegance in Cheng culture. It is said that one flew overhead at the time of Chen's birth, and his mother named him for it. He rose from poverty to become emperor of his people, and he was loved by many but despised by some. He was warrior, general, husband, father, poet, philosopher, painter, but most of all he was enemy to the machinations of the shamans who tried to secretly govern all aspects of the people.

Cheng: *Chg.* "Warrior." The overall name of the various related tribes united by Chen Fei. It was a word for warrior in his dialect, later adopted for his growing army and last of all for the people of his nation. His empire disintegrated after his assassination, but much of the culture he fostered endured.

Cheng Empire: A vast array of realms formerly governed by kings and united, briefly, under Chen Fei. One of the largest empires ever to rise in Alithoras.

Conclave of Shamans: The government of the shamans, consisting of several elders and their chosen assistants.

Cragamasta: *Chg.* "The bull that charges." A god of the Cheng pantheon, associated with war, battle and thunderstorms.

Dakashul: *Chg.* "Stallion of two colors – a piebald." Chief of the Iron Dog Clan.

Dastrin: *Chg.* "Shadow of the forest." Warrior of the Silent Owl Clan, and cousin to the chief. With Shar's help, elevated to the chieftainship.

Duthenor: A tribe on the other side of the Eagle Claw Mountains, unrelated to the Cheng. They are breeders of cattle and herders of sheep. Said to be great warriors, and rumor holds that Asana is partly of their blood.

Eagle Claw Mountains: A mountain range toward the south of the Cheng Empire. It is said the people who later became the Cheng lived here first and over centuries moved out to populate the surrounding lands. Others believe that these people were blue-eyed, and intermixed with various other races as they came down off the mountains to trade and make war.

Elù-haraken: *Hal.* "The shadowed wars." Long ago battles in a time that is become myth to the Cheng tribes.

Fen Wolf Tribe: A tribe that live in Tsarin Fen. Once, they and the neighboring Soaring Eagle Tribe were one people and part of a kingdom. It is also told that Chen Fei was born in that realm.

Fields of Rah: Rah signifies "ocean of the sky" in many Cheng dialects. It is a country of vast grasslands but at its center is Nagrak City, which of old was the capital of the empire. It was in this city that the emperor was assassinated.

Gan: *Chg.* "They who have attained." It is an honorary title added to a person's name after they have acquired great skill. It can be applied to warriors, shamans, sculptors, weavers or any particular expertise. It is reserved for the greatest of the best.

Go Shan: *Chg.* "Daughter of wisdom." An epithet of Shulu Gan.

Great Oath: A promise or pledge, bound by magic, invented during the Shadowed Wars. If broken, it is said the swearers sicken and die, killed by their own magic.

Green Hornet Clan: A grassland clan immediately to the west of the Wahlum Hills. Their numbers are relatively small, but they are famous for their use of venomed arrows and especially darts.

Halathrin: *Hal.* "People of Halath." A race of elves named after an honored lord who led an exodus of his people to the land of Alithoras in pursuit of justice, having sworn to defeat a great evil. They are human, though of fairer form, greater skill and higher culture. They possess a unity of body, mind and spirit that enables insight and endurance beyond the native races of Alithoras. Said to be immortal, but killed in great numbers during their conflicts in ancient times with the evil they sought to destroy. Those conflicts are collectively known as the Shadowed Wars.

Heart of the Hurricane: The shamans' term for the state of mind warriors call Stillness in the Storm. See that term for further information.

Huigar: *Chg.* "Mist on the mountain peak." A bodyguard to Shar. Daughter of the chief of the Smoking Eyes Clan, and a swordsperson of rare skill.

Iron Dog Clan: A tribe of the Wahlum Hills. So named for their legendary endurance and determination.

Kubodin: *Chg.* Etymology unknown. A wild warrior from the Wahlum Hills, and chief of the Two Ravens Clan. Simple appearing, but far more than he seems. Asana's manservant and friend.

Leaping Deer Tribe: A clan of the Nahlim Forest.

Leng Fah: *Chg.* "Wolf skills." An organization of warrior scouts who patrol the borders of Tsarin Fen to protect its people from hostile incursions by other tribes. They take their name from the swamp wolf, a creature of great stealth and cunning. This is the totem animal of the Fen Wolf tribe.

Lòhren: *Hal. Prn.* Ler-ren. "Knowledge giver – a counselor." Other terms used by various nations include sage, wizard, and druid.

Mach Furr: *Hal.* "The mists of nothingness." Magic whereby the user passes into the void, not just in spirit but in body. It is perilous, ill understood, and used but rarely. Also called Traveling.

Magic: Mystic power.

Maklar: *Chg.* "Tall antlers." Chief of the Roaring Stag Tribe.

Malach Gan: *Chg.* "Pearl of many colors, plus the honorary gan – master." A lòhren and a shaman of ancient times. Perhaps still living.

Master Kaan: *Chg.* "Peace of a mountain valley." Abbot of the Nashwan Temple.

Nachtar: *Chg.* "Boar with one tusk." Shaman of the Roaring Stag Tribe.

Nahring: *Chg.* "White on the lake – mist." Chief of the Smoking Eyes Clan, and father of Huigar. Rumor persists that his family possesses some kind of magic, but if so it has never been publicly revealed.

Nagrading: *Chg.* "Those who return triumphant." One of the chief trainers of the nazram in Nagrak City.

Nagrak: *Chg.* "Those who follow the herds." A Cheng tribe that dwell on the Fields of Rah. Traditionally they lived a nomadic lifestyle, traveling in the wake of herds of wild cattle that provided all their needs. But an element of their tribe, and some contend this was another tribe in origin that they conquered, are great builders and live in a city.

Nagrak City: A great city at the heart of the Fields of Rah. Once the capital of the Cheng Empire.

Nahat: *Chg.* "A gathering of fifty." A group of shamans splintered away from the shaman order.

Nahat-nitra: *Chg.* A gathering of fifty swords - a battalion.

Nahlim Forest: *Chg.* "Green mist." An ancient forest in the west of Cheng lands.

Nakatath: *Chg.* "Emperor-to-be." A term coined by Chen Fei and used by him during the period where he sought to bring the Cheng tribes together into one nation. It is said that it deliberately mocked the shamans, for they used the term *Nakolbrin* to signify an apprentice shaman ready to ascend to full authority.

Nashwan Temple: *Chg.* "Place of rocks." A holy temple in the region of Nashwan in the Skultic Mountains.

Nazram: *Chg.* "The wheat grains that are prized after the chaff is excluded." An elite warrior organization that is in service to the shamans. For the most part, they are selected from those who quest for the twin swords each triseptium, though there are exceptions to this.

Nightbringer Canyons: Deep canyons in the far west of the Cheng lands.

Night Walker Clan: A tribe of the Wahlum Hills. The name derives from their totem animal, which is a nocturnal predator of thick forests. It's a type of cat, small but fierce and covered in black fur.

Nogrod: *Chg.* "Aisle of tree trunks." Chief of the Leaping Deer Tribe.

Nomak: *Chg.* "Straight beam – usually refers to a pine tree." A warrior of the Roaring Stag Tribe.

Olekhai: *Chg.* "The falcon that plummets." A famous and often used name in the old world before, and during, the Cheng Empire. Never used since the assassination of the emperor, however. The most prominent bearer of the name during the days of the emperor was the chief of his council of wise men. He was, essentially, prime minister of the emperor's government. But he betrayed his lord and his people. Shulu Gan spared his life, but only so as to punish him with a terrible curse.

Quest of Swords: Occurs every triseptium to mark the three times seven years the shamans lived in exile during the emperor's life. The best warriors of each clan seek the twin swords of the emperor. Used by the shamans as a means of finding the most skilled warriors in the land and recruiting them to their service.

Radatan: *Chg.* "The ears that flick – a slang term for deer." A hunter of the Two Ravens Clan.

Ravengrim: One of the elders of the Nahat.

Roaring Stag Tribe: A Cheng tribe located in the Nahlim Forest.

Runeguard: One of the elders of the Nahat.

Shadowed Wars: See Elù-haraken.

Shaman: The religious leaders of the Cheng people. They are sorcerers, and though the empire is fragmented they work as one across the lands to serve their own united purpose. Their spiritual home is Three Moon Mountain, but few save shamans have ever been there.

Shar: *Chg.* "White stone – the peak of a mountain." A young woman of the Fen Wolf Tribe. Claimed by Shulu Gan to be the descendent of Chen Fei.

Shulu Gan: *Chg.* The first element signifies "magpie." A name given to the then leader of the shamans for her hair was black, save for a streak of white that ran through it.

Silent Owl Tribe: A Cheng tribe located in the Nahlim Forest.

Skultic Mountains: Skultic means "the bones that do not speak." It is a reference to the rocky terrain. The mountains rise up in proximity to the Nahlim Forest.

Smoking Eyes Clan: A tribe of the Wahlum Hills. Named for a god, who they take as their totem.

Soaring Eagle Tribe: A tribe that borders the Fen Wolf clan. At one time, one with them, but now, as is the situation with most tribes, hostilities are common. The eagle is their totem, for the birds are plentiful in the mountain lands to the south and often soar far from their preferred habitat over the tribe's grasslands.

Stillness in the Storm: The state of mind a true warrior seeks in battle. Neither angry nor scared, neither hopeful nor worried. When emotion is banished from the mind, the body is free to express the skill acquired through long years of training. Sometimes also called Calmness in the Storm or the Heart of the Hurricane.

Sun Lo River: *Chg.* "White thunder." A river originating in the Eagle Claw Mountains that, along with the mountains, helps define the southern border of Cheng lands.

Svathkin: *Chg.* "Piebald hide." Shaman of the Silent Owl Tribe.

Swimming Osprey Clan: A tribe of the Wahlum Hills. Their totem is the osprey, often seen diving into the ocean to catch fish.

Taga Nashu: *Chg.* "The Grandmother who does not die." One of the many epithets of Shulu Gan, greatest of the shamans but cast from their order.

Tagayah: Origin of name unknown. A creature of magic and chaos, born in the old world long before even the Shadowed Wars, but used during those conflicts by the forces of evil.

Targesha: *Chg.* "Emerald serpent." Chief of the Green Hornet Tribe.

Three Moon Mountain: A mountain in the Eagle Claw range. Famed as the home of the shamans. None know what the three moons reference relates to except, perhaps, the shamans.

Traveling: Magic of the highest order. It enables movement of the physical body from one location to another via entry to the void in one place and exit in a different. Only the greatest magicians are capable of it, but it is almost never used. The risk of death is too high. But use of specially constructed rings of standing stones makes it safer.

Triseptium: A period of three times seven years. It signifies the exiles of the shamans during the life of the emperor. Declared by the shamans as a cultural treasure, and celebrated by them. Less so by the tribes, but the shamans encourage it. Much more popular now than in past ages.

Tsarin Fen: *Chg.* Tsarin, which signifies mountain cat, was a general under Chen Fei. It is said he retired to the swamp after the death of his leader. At one time, many regions and villages were named after generals, but the shamans changed the names and did all they could to make people forget the old ones. In their view, all who served the emperor were criminals and their achievements were not to be celebrated. Tsarin Fen is one of the few such names that still survive.

Two Ravens Clan: A tribe of the Wahlum Hills. Their totem is the raven.

Uhrum: *Chg.* "The voice that sings the dawn." Queen of the gods.

Wahlum Hills: *Chg. Comb. Hal.* "Mist-shrouded highlands." Hills to the north-west of the old Cheng empire, and home to Kubodin.

Wolfshadow: An elder of the Nahat. As is common among the Nahat, names are taken from outside the Cheng lands. Usually, but not always, they derive from contact with Duthenor tribesmen. There are exceptions, but the names often relate to battle. The Nahat see themselves as warriors rather than just users of magic.

About the author

I'm a man born in the wrong era. My heart yearns for faraway places and even further afield times. Tolkien had me at the beginning of *The Hobbit* when he said, ". . . one morning long ago in the quiet of the world . . ."

Sometimes I imagine myself in a Viking mead-hall. The long winter night presses in, but the shimmering embers of a log in the hearth hold back both cold and dark. The chieftain calls for a story, and I take a sip from my drinking horn and stand up . . .

Or maybe the desert stars shine bright and clear, obscured occasionally by wisps of smoke from burning camel dung. A dry gust of wind marches sand grains across our lonely campsite, and the wayfarers about me stir restlessly. I sip cool water and begin to speak.

I'm a storyteller. A man to paint a picture by the slow music of words. I like to bring faraway places and times to life, to make hearts yearn for something they can never have, unless for a passing moment.

Printed in Great Britain
by Amazon